BEV Lapp

W9-CFO-771

GLORY in the FLOWER

NORMA JOHNSTON

TEMPO BOOKS, NEW YORK

This Tempo Book contains the complete
text of the original hardcover edition.

GLORY IN THE FLOWER

A Tempo Book / published by arrangement with
Atheneum Publishers

PRINTING HISTORY
Tempo edition / October 1981
Second printing / April 1983

ISBN: 0-441-29399-9

Tempo Books are published by Charter Communications, Inc.,
200 Madison Avenue, New York, New York 10016.
Tempo Books are registered in the United States Patent Office.
PRINTED IN THE UNITED STATES OF AMERICA

Contents

Though nothing can bring back the hour
Of splendour in the grass, of glory in the flower;
We will grieve not, rather find
Strength in what remains behind.

William Wordsworth

CHAPTER ONE

January

My name is Tish Sterling, and I live on Bryant Avenue, in West Farms, The Bronx, New York. I may as well list these bald facts straight off and get them over with, since henceforth I intend to avoid what Mrs. Owens, my English teacher, refers to as the "I-syndrome." Having read over my old Journal about a week ago, I have come to the definite conclusion that my writing suffers from an overabundance of me-me-me.

I begin this new Journal, otherwise known as The Tears and Trials of Letitia Chambers Sterling, with an account of New Year's Day, 1901, just in time to record my family and friends, in regrettably characteristic form, at the Lathams' open house, the opening of Pa's secretarial school, and the metamorphosis of the Browning Society. Around our neighborhood, crises usually do seem to occur in threes.

The first crisis got off with a bang, or maybe I should say a screech, at the lunch table on New Year's Day. Mama hasn't made much holiday fuss this year, since we're still recuperating from my sister Bronwyn's wedding on Christmas Eve. Gramps only departed for his Pennsylvania farm a day ago, and Mama is looking forward to getting the kids back to school and putting up her feet in a quiet house, which means that lunch on New Year's was long on leftovers and short on style. It was supposed to feature leftover roast beef, but Mama, who isn't used yet to Bron's not being around to help, made the mistake of leaving the roast beef unguarded on the table. When she returned, half the roast was already inside Cicero, our almost-sheepdog, who was looking idiotically pleased with himself, and the other half was leaking juice on the Oriental rug.

"Hell and damn!" Mama yelled, an expression she has picked up lately from my thirteen-year-old sister Marnie. "Tarnation children can't take responsibility for anything without I tell you three times! All the thanks I get! Pa not home again when I need him! Me in this condition!"

Since we're so used to these speeches that we can even chime in on the chorus, we don't usually pay overmuch attention. But today's was loud and genuine enough to bring us all running, even Ben, my older brother, who first had to take time to snuff out the roll-your-own he'd been smoking in the privacy of the attic. Ben dragged Cicero outside and tied him up, Marnie cleaned the carpet since Mama was in no shape to bend down and do it, I decided Mama could benefit from a cup of tea, and Peter, who often manages to sound like he's forty instead of eight, said, "Actually, a dog's saliva is sanitary, so it shouldn't really harm the meat a bit."

"Don't give two hoots," Mama said firmly. "None of us touching that roast now, and that's for sure." Only at that moment she got a look under the table and there was Missy, who's still only four and capitalizes on it, sitting on the table stretcher gnawing contentedly away on the roast-beef bone.

Mama had two choices, hysteria or laughter. Fortunately she chose the latter. She collapsed into the nearest chair and laughed till the tears rolled down her cheeks. "Don't know why I bother trying to live civilized," she gasped, wiping her eyes. "Waste of effort on this pack of heathens. Oh, well. Least your Pa's not home. All ate too much over the holidays anyway. Can fill up at the Lathams' later."

"I can go down to the delicatessen and get you something, if you want," Ben offered solicitously. "Don't forget, Ma, you're eating for two."

"Don't remind me," Mama retorted. "Can see through that anyway. Let you out, you'll forget to come home, run into Doug Latham somewhere and the two of you take off for the day. Emma Jane wouldn't thank me none if you drag her eldest son away, day she's giving a party." Which is just like Mama, casting aspersions on whatever altruistic motives we chance to have.

Ben scowled and went off to sneak the rest of his cigarette, Marnie muttered something about fat chance Doug would help his mother anyway, which is the absolute truth, and I decided this was an excellent time to seek out some solitude upstairs and start my Journal.

Now that Bron's married I have our bedroom to myself, except when Melissa crawls in with me. Missy's supposed to be sharing with Marnie down the hall, but she's given to transferring locations during her nocturnal wanderings, and this can be disastrous, because she still has occasional accidents in her sleep.

"Don't see why you don't move in with Tish now," Mama said to Marnie. "Make more sense. One year apart in age. Dry bed."

"Between wet beds with Missy, and catfights with Tish, I'll risk the wet bed," Marnie said firmly. "It's the lesser of two evils, Mama."

It still feels strange and lonely having the bedroom to myself, although it is going to be undeniably convenient when it comes to burning the after-midnight oil with nobody knowing. Snug beneath three quilts while the winds howl outside and the apple tree taps ghostly fingers against the bow window, I can write in my Journal, write extra-credit compositions, write stories. Entering high school opened a new world for me—for the first time I'm not considered weird because I love Shakespeare, history, poetry; because I have a habit of feeling everything too deeply. Both Mr. Grimes, our Greek-god history teacher, and Mrs. Owens encourage me to pretty much follow my own fancy, although they come down hard on such sordid details as organization, quality, and style. I have finally stopped writing about Balkan princesses, haunted mansions, and other things beyond my own experience, and lately my compositions have leaned heavily on anecdotes pumped from Gramps and on other incidents, which happened closer to home. Mama got pretty mad when she found out I'd done one on the time Ben and Marnie got Pa drunk by serving him year-old cider, even though I got A+ and the classroom rocked with laughter.

As a matter of fact, my grades could benefit from a few extra-credit items right now, since my mind during the month of December was decidedly not on school. But I wasn't in the mood for thinking about that on New Year's Day. Up in the door-shut privacy of my room, I took out the new notebook with its tantalizingly empty pages. It, like the one I used from June through December, had been given to me by my best friend, Celinda Dodds.

I was about to make a serious start on this Journal, befitting New Year's and new leaves, when I heard the front door slam, and the sound of voices indicated that Pa was home. I ambled downstairs just in time to hear him say, "Oh, drat it, Evie, I forgot all about that shindig at the Lathams'. You take the children and go along without me. I really have to work on things for the school."

Pa's new secretarial school was opening on the morrow and he was jittery as a June bug waiting for the day to come. He'd been down to the office building all day, shifting desks around for the umpteenth time, and Mama, who doesn't like being left alone on a holiday, sniffed. "Not going without an escort. Feel like a conspicuous fool in my condition." She was forgetting that everybody'd seen her at the wedding last week, her head high and eyes snapping, just daring them to find anything amusing in an *enceinte* mother of the bride. "Think you might consider me. Cooped up in the house all week. Need some recreation." She stopped, took a good look at Pa's tired eyes, and changed her tune.

"Guess it would be nice, having a quiet afternoon, just the two of us," Mama allowed in the grumpy tone she has when she's feeling gentle. "Children can go alone. Or stay home. Been doing a lot of socializing lately."

"Ben can take us," I interjected firmly, having no intention of letting the day go by without seeing Ken Latham, and went off to remind my brother that he owed me a few favors. And that is how it happened that we went to the Lathams' soirée without parental escort, which, in view of later occurrences, is probably just as well.

When we arrived, the party was in full swing. Mr. Latham is the kind of man, as Ben once said, who never made the football team, ended up as its water boy, and ever since has managed to give the impression that he was the star. His wife is a faded, pretty woman who is given to frequent sighing, a thing which, considering the character of her eldest son, Doug,

I can fully understand. Their other son, is altogether different, as I have good reason to know. We paid our respects to the adults in the parlor and joined the kids in the kitchen. Most of the neighborhood crowd had already arrived, and Doug was holding forth in his usual form.

Ken was there too, and he hadn't heard us come in. He was sitting quietly in a back corner, looking at his brother. Seeing Ken that way, without his knowing it, gave me a queer feeling. This was the first I'd seen him as I used to before last summer when I really got to know him, seen him as the world still sees him—Kenny, the younger Latham kid, the quiet one, lost in his brother's shadow. For a moment it made me genuinely angry, that all that Kenneth was could be so dimmed by all that Doug wasn't. Then Ken looked up and saw me and grinned, and the moment of awareness was over, and he was again the Kenneth that I knew.

I wondered how I had looked to him in that split second before our eyes had met. Had he seen what I knew too well was the familiar image—Tish Sterling, Bronwyn's plain little sister, with the dirty blonde hair and the skin that almost matched, childishly thin and without even as much shape as her eighth-grade sister, for goodness sake? Tish Sterling, the melodramatic one, the stubborn one? Or could he by some miracle see the other person shut away inside, the person I was half too shy to show even to him? He must see something other people haven't, because the whole neighborhood knows he is my beau.

This is the New Year's resolution I am going to keep for sure, I decided firmly; I am going to let more of the inside come out if it kills us all.

"I was wondering whether you kids were coming," Ken said, joining us.

"We never miss free eats," Ben said, with devastating frankness. "Surprised you could even see us in this mob."

"Yeah," Ken said. It wasn't like him to be so monosyllabic, or so ungrammatical. I looked at him sharply. He was looking at Doug, enthroned on the kitchen table like the King of the Hill. Mrs. Latham darted in, rescued a platter of cold cuts from the table and sidled out, almost apologetically. I could just imagine how Mama would have handled the situation if that had been Ben, and my sentiments agreed with Mama's.

"Doug," Ken said, reading my mind, "is enjoying himself as usual."

"And you?" I asked daringly.

Ken shrugged. "You get used to it," he said ambiguously. What he was referring to I could not be sure.

I shot a venomous look in Doug's direction—and practically expired from shock. Doug had taken a cigarette from his pocket and was ostentatiously lighting up. Most of the boys smoke out behind the barn, and Ben's attic indulgences are well-known, but none of them ever try it in the house; a gentleman is not supposed to offend the delicate sensibilities of ladies with tobacco smoke. Behind me I heard Ben whistle and knew even he thought Doug was going too far as he took a deep drag, tapped off the ashes, and directed a smoke ring at the ceiling, and then another.

There were admiring little *oohs* and *ahs* from the coterie around Doug's feet, the idiots. To my disgust, I saw that Marnie was there among them. Mary Lou Hodge, her curls piled up like something out of the Folies Bergere, was draped seductively across a chair. As Doug wafted the cigarette in her direction, she gave one of her coy little squeals and ·pounced upon it.

Doug regarded her with what he obviously thought were

devilishly wicked half-closed eyes. "You wouldn't dare."

"Wouldn't I?" Mary Lou said archly. To everyone's astonishment she took a deep drag and exhaled without even choking. In the silence she took another puff, extended the cigarette to Doug and batted her eyes. "I'd dare anything you would," she said with meaning.

Ben choked. He may be Doug's best friend, but he is decidedly not impressed with Mary Lou. "Holy Toledo, what does she think she is, Little Egypt?"

"Doug seems to think so."

"Doug's drunk," Ken said flatly. "My father's been having him fix the drinks for the gentlemen, and every time he does, he helps himself. Come on, let's get out of here. I need some fresh air." He turned abruptly and went out the kitchen door, and I followed.

It was cold outside without our coats, but I didn't care. The air was wine-sharp after the staleness of the kitchen, and stars twinkled like chips of ice in the night sky. Ken jammed his hands in his pockets and stared off at them, and I sat on the railing, not knowing what to say. I couldn't tell him his brother is a boor and a moral idiot. I couldn't say Ken is worth ten of Doug, although nobody but me has the sense to see it. I just sat in silence and thanked my stars that Mama wasn't there to notice we were out in the cold alone.

After a while, Ken took a deep breath and muttered, "I suppose we ought to go in," and we wandered back into the kitchen, which had grown more raucous. Just about everybody of school age in the neighborhood was there by now, except for Celinda. Her mother didn't believe in parties. The crowd, as it usually did, had separated into groups. The "nice kids," meaning Anne Cameron and the many Molloys, including my friend Stella, and the Breidenbachs, who lived next door to us, and such were in the pantry having a merry time of it over punch and salads. The hooligans, under the spell of Doug and Mary Lou, were still established in the kitchen. So, to my regret, were Ben and Marnie.

I sidled over to Marnie and muttered, "Mama would cut your throat."

"She'd cut yours, too," Marnie whispered back, shooting a look at the back door. "I won't tell if you won't."

I could have kicked her.

"At least," Marnie added virtuously, "*I'm* not doing anything. I'm only looking."

I only wished I'd gotten a chance to do something, but I couldn't very well say that to my younger sister. Instead I looked, too, at the spectacle of Mary Lou taking a healthy swig from a flask Doug offered her. Apparently they had been continuing their game of Anything You Dare, and the crowd was fascinated. Mary Lou's face was flushed, her hair was falling down, and her clothes were rumpled. I wondered what they'd been up to while Ken and I were out.

"They've been up to plenty," Marnie murmured as if she'd read my mind, "and it wasn't all of it in the kitchen." We looked at each other. "Mary Lou," Marnie said deliberately, "is a pig."

There are times my sister has better sense than I'd have given her credit for.

Other people too were beginning to have had enough. Even the hooligan crowd looked restive. In the parlor the adults were talking too loudly to hear any noises from the kitchen. I heard the strident tones of my Aunt Kate, and hoped to heaven she wouldn't take a notion to amble out. Doug rescued the flask back from Mary Lou, who looked as if she was reaching the sheep-drunk stage, sloppy and sleepy. Doug was obviously still in the lion stage, roaring and showing every sign of eventually turning into swine.

"Now this," he proclaimed boozily, taking another snort, "is more like it. More like a party. Anybody else want a party? How about you, Mary Loulou?"

Mary Lou pulled herself awake and mumbled something that sounded like, "Sure, Dougie honey."

"You and me," Doug pronounced carefully, laboring over the words and practically falling into her lap, "know what a good time is. Not like those ol' fossils." He jerked a contemptuous head in the direction of the parlor. "They don't know how to have a lil old good time. Suppose we show 'em."

He lowered himself carefully to his feet, and with great precision bent over and produced another, full bottle from a kitchen cupboard. "Suppose," he suggested with an air of confidential conspiracy, "we show 'em how to make a real party punch. Not tell and see what happens. Do you dare, Mary Loulou? Do you dare?"

Mary Lou, with a struggle, drew herself erect. "I dare anything you dare," she enunciated with care. "I thought I showed you that."

"Sure you have," Doug said approvingly, and passed her the bottle. "Go ahead."

The air in the kitchen was electric with silence. I knew exactly what every kid there, hooligans included, was feeling —embarrassment, and disgust, and something like dismay. And a wish that somebody, anybody, would walk into the kitchen and stop the thing that was happening before it was too late. I knew too that not one of us, myself included, had the guts to walk out of that room and get a grown-up. The code, although unwritten, was too strong. There were kids, and there were parents, and you didn't betray one to the other, no matter what.

Then behind me I heard a quiet voice say, "No," and it was Ken.

Doug couldn't believe his ears. "Waddja say, lil brother?" he inquired, swaying forward.

Ken's face was white, and a little muscle twitched in his cheek as he repeated, "I said no. Don't do it, Doug. It will ruin Mother's party, and besides, there are folks here who don't drink."

"Ol' fossils an' babies," Doug said. "Like you, Kenny baby. You gonna stop me, huh? You haven't got the guts. Go back an' play baby games with your lil baby girl friend." His contemptuous eyes raked up and down my body, and I felt exactly as if he had stripped me naked. "Lil prissy baby Goody Two-Shoes, don't know anything except how to put her nose in a book. Just like you." Doug draped his arm around Mary Lou, who melted against him, and leered at his brother. "Wouldn't know what to do with a real girl, would you? An' you think you're gonna tell me what to do, Kenny baby?"

I scarcely saw what happened, because to my shame I had retreated into the red mist of my humiliation. All I knew was that suddenly Ken's arm had swung out, and the bottle had been knocked from Doug's hand, and Ken's fist had connected against his brother's face.

Thank goodness alcohol slows people's reactions down. It took a few seconds for Doug to realize just what had happened, and in those seconds Ben had grabbed him from behind. Ben was saying soothingly, "Forget these babies, Doug. This is no fun. Let's go outside, just us guys, and have a smoke." And he was steering Doug firmly out the back door.

"I think," Marnie said clearly, "it's time we all got out of here." And in silent embarrassment, everybody did, not looking at each other, leaving Ken and me alone together with Mary Lou, who had collapsed into oblivion in a kitchen chair.

Ken and I stood there and couldn't face each other. Something that had been precious between us had been cheapened for us both. For the rest of my life, I thought, when Kenneth looks at me he's going to see me with Doug's eyes. I turned away, pressing the back of my hand hard against my mouth.

"I'm sorry," Ken said in a whisper. "I should have stopped him sooner. I should have jammed that first cigarette down his rotten throat."

"Don't," I said painfully. "I know why you couldn't. And it's—not for the reasons he said."

There was another silence, and then Ken came over and stood behind me. So close, and yet there was such a barrier in that small space between us, and I knew Ken couldn't bridge it any more than I could turn around and meet his eyes. I wondered if we were ever going to be able to again. I hate you, Douglas Latham, I thought silently.

Then Ken reached out, and hesitated, and let his hands come to rest gently on my shoulders. "Thanks," he said awkwardly. "For—well, for knowing."

And I knew that it was going to be all right, that I was the inner Tish to him, just as he was that other Kenneth. But no more in innocence, never again with that same purity of focus we had had before.

Ben came in and said, "I sobered him up under the outdoor pump. He's out in the barn. He'll be all right now." He slapped Ken in comradely fashion on the shoulder, and rounded up Marnie who was in the parlor being polite to our Aunt Kate, and we said our good-bys and started home in silence.

We didn't want to talk; we didn't need to agree that we would spill no word of these events at home. That was a foregone conclusion. I knew we would never even discuss them among ourselves. But when we got home, after we'd told our parents that it was a lovely party and that the Lathams were sorry they hadn't come, after I was up in my own room getting undressed and trying not to look at my body's immature reflection in the mirror, my sister Marnie came in.

"Thought I'd sleep in here tonight, if it's all right with you," she said casually, and kept up a steady stream of nonsense until long after the light was out.

But later, much later, after Marnie was asleep, I still lay wakeful, staring out at the cold bleak chips of ice in the night sky. I had never admired Kenneth so much, nor been quite so confused at my own feelings.

I certainly thought Doug Latham had all the moral sensibilities of an alley cat; in fact, Aunt Kate's tom was more fastidious. I did believe—for all I pretended to mock them on occasion—in the code of values my parents had passed on to me.

Why, then, when the very moral values I believed in were put into Doug's words, did they sound so contemptible and wrong? And why, quite suddenly and clearly, did it matter so terribly to me how I was thought of by somebody whom I myself despised?

CHAPTER TWO

January

Mary Lou had a ripsnorting headache for the next three days, and it served her right. I do not know what she told her mother as an excuse for staying home from school. Doug Latham was out of school, too, but he was cutting. It was kind of nice not having the two of them around.

As a matter of fact, it was even nice getting back to school again after vacation. The air was full of the smell of new beginnings. After school was dismissed at three, the usual little crowd of Celinda and Anne and Stella and me congregated in the English classroom, bringing Mrs. Owens and Mr. Grimes up to date on our holiday happenings. And that was good, too, because Kenneth joined us, so our first facing of each other after those embarrassing moments in his kitchen did not have to take place in awkward private.

Mr. Grimes had news, too. "There's going to be a reorganization meeting of the Browning Society Friday afternoon, for everyone who was inducted into membership before—er, shall we say, before its temporary disbandment last September."

I became very busy scribbling silly messages on the blackboard, but I could very well feel everybody's eyes upon me.

That disbandment had been at the express wishes of Mr. Moore, the principal, and it had come about as a result of a moment of truth between Mary Lou and me. At the end of the moment of truth, I, a newly created member of the Browning Society, had resigned.

"The officers met with Mr. Grimes and Mr. Moore and me over vacation," Mrs. Owens said. "It is their intention to reorganize along more democratic lines. Hold an evening party open to anyone interested, followed by membership candidates submitting samples of their writing. Or perhaps have an essay contest held after school, with results to be assessed by a panel of judges. With the authors' names not attached, of course."

Since Mrs. Owens does not normally go around sounding like a walking textbook, I knew perfectly well she was up to something. I shot a sharp glance in Mr. Grimes's direction, but his face was bland.

Celinda rescued me from my discomfiture. "Well," she said, sliding off the desk on which she had been perched, "I don't know about the rest of you, but if I don't get home before four o'clock I'll be drawn and quartered."

"Golly, so will I," Ken said. "I promised my dad I'd help him at the store." So he took off in the direction of town and his father's feed and grain store, and the rest of us started towards home. I was grateful to Celinda for keeping a conversation going, for Stella was dying of curiosity about the Browning Society incident, and she has the perseverance of a trial lawyer once she gets started. Stella had moved to our neighborhood after it all happened last fall. But after we'd said good-by to Anne and Stella and were walking along Bryant Avenue through lightly falling snow, Celinda turned to me squarely, and her eyes were twinkling.

"Well," she said, "what are you going to do about it?"

"About what?"

"About you know perfectly well what. You wiped the dust of the Browning Society off your feet last fall because Mary Lou blackballed Hodel Resnikov on account of she was too different and too smart. But Hodel's gone now, and apparently Mary Lou's getting her comeuppance about that plagiarized poem that got *her* into membership. At any rate, she knows the whole world knows about it, thanks to you."

"Don't remind me."

"Don't be silly. Everybody knows you only tattled accidentally because you were so blamed mad, and anyway it was a good thing that you did. The point is, what are you going to do now? Make a crusade out of not being a member, or come back in?"

"I don't know yet."

Celinda hesitated. "I wish you would come back," she said at last. "I know it's a snob group, and I'm not a real writer, not like you are, anyway. But—oh, drat it, Tish, it meant something to me to be asked to join. And I'll be scared to death to go if you're not there."

"You can go with Stella. She's bound to join."

"I'm scared to death of her, too, sometimes," Celinda admitted frankly.

I will not go into my emotions or motivations, because I do not particularly want to delve into them myself. Suffice to say that when Ken said to me on Friday, "Wait for me after school and we can walk to the meeting together," I did not say him nay.

Braced by the security of his presence beside me, I steeled myself to walk into the meeting in the school library. This was a classroom, actually, which had been converted by the addition of bookshelves, a center table, and an assortment of chairs. Nearly all the erstwhile members of the Browning Society were lounging in them now, but to my relief I did not meet the speculative looks I was anticipating. Everybody was too busy. Mr. Grimes had them all at work on plans for the projected evening party. The fact that he had gotten authorization for it to be in the evening was a coup; everyone in school would express passionate interest in joining anything that would get them out of the house on a school night. Mr. Grimes can be a regular Machiavelli when he chooses.

The date of the party was set for the following Thursday night. It was supposed to be called an "open meeting," in order to impress parents with its seriousness of purpose, but everybody knew what was really meant. At a quarter to five our planning meeting was dismissed, and Kenneth walked me home.

"Well?" he asked me quizzically, exactly as Celinda had done.

"Well what?"

"Well what you've been asking yourself all afternoon. Are you going to or not?"

"I don't know yet. I haven't had time to think."

"You've got a week," Ken said, and we parted at my gate.

I knew what he meant. If I went to that party, everybody would know I was back as a member again. But I didn't really need the week to think, no matter what I'd said. I needed it to come to terms with myself. For the plain fact was that I knew, as I had known since last September, that I would die before allowing myself to be permanently cut off from the Browning Society. I intended to be a writer; I couldn't bear to be an outsider, or a follower, rather than a leader. And in our school, for anyone of brains or talent, the Browning Society was where the status lay.

I didn't want to go into the ethics of the situation with anybody, least of all myself. It was just the way things were. Machiavelli would have had a word for it, I thought, and went into the house to be met by Mama with her finger at her lips.

"Don't wake your Pa. Taking a nap in the study."

"Pa's home already?"

"Friday. For once, soon's the students departed, he did too." Mama grinned. "Guess he's finding out teaching school's not such a picnic as he thought."

"Neither is going to school," I said. "As I could have told him." I followed Mama to the kitchen where she poured us each a cup of tea and cut a piece of pound cake. "Might as well," she said. "Not going to have supper till your Pa wakes of his own accord."

Marnie joined us, helped herself liberally to cake, and inquired what had occurred that day to flatten Pa.

"Viney Hodge," Mama said. "Showed up at the school to enroll for the legal secretarial course. Wearing one of those new peekaboo shirtwaists with her corset showing, and a lot more besides. Your Aunt Kate almost expired from shock." Aunt Kate was acting as registrar for Pa's new school.

"The thought of Viney Hodge as a legal secretary," Marnie said, "is a vision straight out of one of those penny dreadful novels she's always reading."

Mama's eyes twinkled. "Guess maybe she's planning on nabbing a lawyer as a husband just like Bron did."

Marnie choked. "Mrs. Evie Stryker Sterling, you're a cat!"

"Can't help if it's the plain truth," Mama said, and got up to take a look at her Stretchable Stew.

On Monday Pa came home to say he'd posted a list of rules and regulations on the wall of the school. "Including one saying peekaboo waists are not allowed. I hadn't expected such regulations would be necessary for young ladies, high school graduates, working towards business careers."

"Weren't expecting Viney Hodge, either," was Mama's comment.

Pa was not the only one who was finding school becoming rapidly burdensome. Somehow I always forgot, in the first flush of getting back to school after vacation, how soon the glow wears off. On Tuesday Mr. Grimes assigned a major research project. "And I don't mean airy flights of fancy, either," he warned. "I mean solid scholarship. Footnotes. Bibliographies. Bear in mind it will count for half your grade this marking period."

In English Mrs. Owens started harping on grammar and spelling and sentence structure, a thing that drives me wild with boredom. So long as you know how to put a sentence together, which I certainly do, although I don't always bother, why do you have to know the rules behind it? In Latin, Sourpuss Sadie was her usual poisonous self, and most of my other subjects managed to be equally obnoxious. The result was that by Thursday night, all students who could make even a pretense of literary interest were agog over the Browning Society party as a welcome respite in the academic maze.

My dearest friends were driving me crazy, too, and I was beginning to kick myself. When the whole thing first came up, why hadn't I just said matter-of-factly, "Well, Browning Society's a whole different organization now," or, "It's only fair, after I was so critical, to come back now and try to make it better"? Instead I'd allowed my outward indecision to take on the tones of a big moral issue, and now I was hoist on my own petard.

I did try the latter reason out on Stella on the way home from school, and she just said, "Oh," equivocally. There was a quizzical look in Ken's eyes, too. Sometimes I think he knows me far too well. He didn't say anything, but when we reached my gate he stopped and hung around until Stella got the message that three was a crowd and said good-by and went on home. I wondered what was coming.

What came was, "Since you've decided to help the Browning Society out, may I stop by and walk you to the meeting?"

I was enormously glad he wanted to, especially since the awkward memory of Doug's drunken insults still hung between us. But I knew perfectly well Mama would not allow it, not without a chaperone. I should have just said so, plainly and simply, but too many things muddied the issue—Doug's insinuations, and the way Ken had phrased my justification for attending. What I did say was, "Are you sure it's safe being seen with such a pariah?"

It was meant to be light and funny but it didn't turn out that way. Ken whitened; he must have read in inferences I hadn't meant. He bowed formally, said, "If that's the way you feel about it, I'll withdraw the request," and walked away.

I felt exactly as if a snowball that I'd thrown myself had ricocheted to land squarely in my face.

I went into the house, was rude to Mama who let it pass for once, and a short while later the telephone rang. I made a dive for it, hoping it was Kenneth, but it was Celinda, who'd been home from school that day.

"Where were you?" I asked.

"Sick headache. Stayed up till three working on the research project." Celinda plunged directly to the purpose of her call. "Are you going tonight? Because if so, can I go with you? Mama won't let me go alone."

"In that case, of course I'll go." There's nothing like using one's friends for justification of one's own mixed motives.

"Don't do me any favors," Celinda said tartly, and hung up.

I seemed to be batting a thousand today. I hunted up Mama and broached the subject of the Browning Society.

"Back home by ten," Mama said firmly. "Ben take you. *And* bring you home. School night no time for lallygagging."

That latter was a direct reference to Ken, but I did not rise to the bait, for I had no intention of discussing our relationship with Mama. What with Bron's sudden marriage and her own equally unexpected infantication, I suspected Mama had sex on her mind these days. Or, rather, that she feared it was on mine. She knew perfectly well how moonstruck I am where Kenneth is concerned.

Actually, Mama doesn't have to worry about the perils of me and Kenneth being alone together, worse luck. Although Ken can and does hold lengthy, profound, and unembarrassed discussions of the passions of the ancient Greeks, he shows little inclination to put their exploits into personal practice. Maybe that's because of overexposure to the exploits of his brother and Mary Lou, who don't know beans about Greek but seem to know a lot about lust. As for me—even now, remembering, I find myself flushing. When Herbie Willis, Bron's old boyfriend, mistaking me for Bron, had trapped me in the blackness of the pantry closet, he'd taught me a lot more about the vulnerability of my own body than I'd been ready yet to learn from someone I despised.

But Mama doesn't know that, and I have no intention that she ever shall, so I kept my mouth shut and submitted to Mama's insistence that Ben escort me to the Browning Society that evening. It wasn't a bad idea anyway, because a little Browning Society influence, whatever its failings, couldn't help but be an improvement on Ben's usual social circle.

So, after dinner, which was rather dismal on account of Pa

was in a somber mood, I dolled myself up in my coral merino, did up my hair to make me look as old as possible, and ran downstairs to find Ben, who was trying to be ungracious about the whole thing. We went out into the chilly night that threatened sleet. In view of the weather, I wasn't sure Celinda's mother would let her come after all, but when we reached her house she came running out to meet us, pulling her coat on as she came.

"You'll catch your death of cold," I said, quoting one of Mama's favorite clichés.

"No, I won't. I'm hot," Celinda said absently. "I think I've got a fever."

I felt her forehead. "Celinda Dodds, you shouldn't have come."

"Yes, I should. I had to get out of the house. If I hadn't," Celinda said grimly, "there'd have been murder done."

"What's the matter?"

"Mama," Celinda said, "is in one of her hellfire and damnation moods. I hope to goodness if we have to discuss literature tonight it will be something absolutely wicked!"

Ben looked alarmed. "I thought you said this was supposed to be a party!"

"It won't hurt you to imbibe a little culture, too," I informed him.

"If la belle Hodge is an officer of this illustrious organization," Ben said, "culture is the last thing we're apt to be imbibing."

"Maybe she'll quit," Celinda said hopefully. "After your telling the world how she signed her name to a poem she didn't write, Tish, you wouldn't think she'd have the gall to show her face."

"Gall is not a thing Mary Lou is short of," I said glumly.

And I was right. When we reached the school, Mary Lou was there in full feather, and as a matter of fact feathers were about the only adornment she wasn't sporting. She looked more suitably attired for New Year's Eve than for a school function. She was wearing her sister Viney's peekaboo waist; you could see just about everything Mary Lou had, and Mary Lou has plenty. Mrs. Owens did not looked pleased, but she was restraining herself, which was more than Mary Lou was doing. Celinda cringed, and Ben made noises as if he were going to be ill.

As for me, I felt as if I were ill myself, because the first thing I saw when I walked in was that Kenneth was already there and in animated discussion with Stella, who was looking very pretty indeed. It did not help that as we entered there was a lull, that everyone seemed to be staring in my direction. I never should have come, I thought.

What I probably should have done was be gay, be friendly, be mindful of my responsibility as a member to circulate and make newcomers feel at home. That was probably what Stella would have done, and she could have carried it off. What I did was park myself in a corner and wallow in my misery. I was damned if I was going to make a fool of myself the way Mary Lou so often did.

After a while Ken noticed me and came over. "I was wondering," he said, "whether you'd changed your mind about coming, after all." There were a variety of implications that could be read into that, and my mind was all too ready to leap to the wrong ones.

"I scarcely think," I said frigidly, "that I'd be missed."

Ken stared at me in genuine astonishment. "For pity's sake, you sound exactly like Celinda when she's feeling unloved!"

"And don't go around criticizing my best friends!"

The little muscle in Ken's cheek twitched. "Apparently," he said, "you share the prevailing estimate that I cannot do anything right." He walked away, and the next thing I knew Stella had snagged him as her partner in one of the games that Mr. Grimes was organizing.

When will I ever learn, I thought, that other people are vulnerable too. And here I'd been indulging in all that nauseating self-congratulation, lately, on how mature and perceptive I'd become.

I'd been right about one thing, I decided. Having dramatically renounced the Browning Society last fall, I should have stayed out. Or else come back wholeheartedly. I shouldn't have come equivocally as I had. I was an alien, a stranger in the midst. Very well, then, I thought, I shall observe the proceedings with a stranger's eyes. Perhaps at least I shall obtain some literary material from my observations. But I shall remain detached; oh yes, above all else, detached. That way one does not get hurt.

There was, actually, a great deal to observe, if one could achieve the detachment I tried to delude myself that I was feeling. It was interesting to see the two crosscurrents that were at work. On the one hand there was the cordial democracy the Browning Society was striving to encourage, the sociability, the everyone's-welcome atmosphere. On the other hand there was the Society's tradition of excellence and prestige, which translated in practical terms into a snobbish clique. The maneuverings, the machinations that were going on around me were fascinating, but I could have enjoyed them better if I hadn't been sunk in melodrama.

Kenneth didn't come back after my rebuff, and my other friends, rightly interpreting my rotten mood, stayed away too. To my disgust, I must have looked like a real lost soul, because after a while the Browning Society president, who doesn't know me from Adam, came over and asked me to dance. I was so revolted by the realization that I'd looked like a waif in need of rescue that I begged off, saying I had a headache.

I did have an ache, but it wasn't in my head. I sat in the corner by the punch bowl, drew my walls up about me, and meditated on both the ills I had done unto others and the ills done unto me. I will not go into the matter of which list was longer.

There was a steady progression to and from the punch bowl at first, but after Mr. Grimes's icebreakers had gotten well under way, the crowd thinned down. After a while there was nobody left around it but Doug and Mary Lou, who appeared to be taking hilarious pleasure in each other's company. I ignored them ostentatiously. Mama would skin me alive if I let any boy paw me the way Doug was doing, but Mary Lou was definitely making no objection. He had his arms draped around her till she was practically falling in the punch bowl. Presently I caught a flash of the flask that Doug had produced on New Year's Day. I need not mention that the consumption of alcoholic beverages on school property is against all laws, but I just closed my eyes. I had had enough of being the conscience of the school.

"Tish Sterling, what are you doing off in a corner?" It was Mrs. Owens, standing before me with that look she sometimes gets, the one that says she's seeing far too much.

"Sitting," I said baldly.

"Oh," Mrs. Owens said, and gave me that look again, and made no comment but just sat down beside me. I am very fond of Mrs. Owens, but there are times I wish she would just go fly a kite. She embarked on a light conversation designed to probe out why I was in such a rotten mood, and the fact that I had put up walls ten feet tall was not about to dissuade her.

I was rescued by Celinda, who wove her way over and dropped down on the chair beside me. "It's so hot in here," she said vaguely.

"Have some punch to cool off," I advised.

"I just have. Lots. It doesn't seem to help." Celinda touched her throat with her handkerchief and closed her eyes.

Mrs. Owens looked at her sharply, poured herself a cup of punch, and tasted it. Then she poured another cup and made a beeline for Mr. Grimes across the room. He tasted it too, and nodded to her briefly, and the next thing we knew Mrs. Owens was striding purposefully back to the punch bowl. She picked it up, marched with it to the nearest window, which she threw open, and flung the contents of the punch bowl out onto the ground.

The silence in the room was thick enough to cut with a cleaver.

Ben materialized at my side. "Come on," he said. "We're going home."

"Why?"

"Because, to be blunt, you've already been mixed up in enough Browning Society scandal, and there's going to be a real stinker starting any minute. Where's Celinda?"

I pointed. Celinda had missed all the excitement; her head drooped on her hands, and she looked like death warmed over. "We'd better get her home. She's getting sicker by the minute. I don't know what—"

"She'll be all right by tomorrow," Ben said, surveying her wryly. "But you'd better not tell her mother what happened."

"What did happen? *Ben?*"

"Good grief, are you that dumb? Somebody spiked the

punch." Ben correctly interpreted my gimlet-eyed stare and added with disgust, "I'm not that stupid, and I've outgrown thinking it's funny to get folks drunk without their knowing. Come on, get her coat on her and let's get out of here."

He didn't even give me time to say good-by to Kenneth, which all things considered was probably just as well. Between us we carted Celinda home and turned her over to her mother's tender mercies, and I thanked my stars her parents were both too puritanical to recognize the effects of alcohol when they encountered them.

It was not, all in all, the pleasantest evening I had ever spent. I felt uneasy, and I did not know why.

Celinda did not come to school the next day, but when I reached our usual corner Stella was there waiting. She had stayed at the party until the bitter end, and she was as wound up as a Christmas top. "Of all the stupid fool things for anybody to do!" she burst out. "If kids are dumb enough to want to get drunk it's one thing, but to wreck something other people have been working for!"

Actually I agreed with everything she was saying, but there are times when Stella's righteousness can put Aunt Kate's to shame. "Oh, hush," I said crossly. "I've had it up to here with the Browning Society, and my head is splitting."

"All right, if that's the way you feel about it. Where's Celinda?"

"Home with a hangover," I said bluntly. "And if anybody's mean enough to tell her that's what it is, she'll probably kill herself. That is, if her mother doesn't do it to her first."

That silenced even Stella. We went on to school which, predictably, was agog and buzzing. In the hall I encountered Kenneth, who fell into step beside me, and we went into the assembly room together. I took one look at his face and my heart almost burst with gratitude. Ken was no longer mad at me. He was somber and preoccupied, and something was obviously troubling him, but it wasn't me. I felt like shouting secret alleluiahs.

The opening exercises proceeded as usual through the flag salute, the reading of a Psalm and the Lord's Prayer; but then, as the usual ripple of movement started through the throng, Mr. Moore rose and walked to the edge of the platform, and the ripple quickly stilled. He surveyed the student body in silence for a moment, and I had never known that he could be so angry. When he spoke, his voice was very quiet.

"Most of you already know what happened here last night," he said. "At a school event for which many students and two faculty members had been working very hard, somebody saw fit to enliven the proceedings by spiking the punch. I understand many of you feel, with the perpetrators, that this was very amusing. I am here to tell you that it is not. It was irresponsible in the highest degree, done with no thought of its effects upon others and upon the school as a whole." His eyes roved the silent crowd. "If there is any, *any* further sign of this sort of irresponsibility—consumption of alcohol or cigarettes on school property, firecrackers, acts of vandalism—all extracurricular activities, athletic, intellectual, and social, will immediately be terminated. Permanently. In a moment, you will be dismissed, and I expect you to go to your classes quietly and get down to work with no discussion of what has taken place. I also expect anyone who has any knowledge of the perpetrators' identity to come to me at the earliest opportunity with that information. Otherwise I will hold them equally responsible for what has happened."

At that moment, as sometimes happens, a picture sprang unbidden to my mind. Doug Latham with his arms draped around Mary Lou's yielding body, bent in conspiratorial laughter above the punch bowl, and the flash of light on the metal of a pocket flask. Doug had had that flask on New Year's Day. Doug had dared Mary Lou then to spike the punch, and Mary Lou had said she would follow where he led.

Ken had remembered; he hadn't seen, but he had remembered; that was why he was so disturbed today. But he had no proof. Only I had seen.

It was circumstantial evidence, my mind said in dialogue with itself. I had no way of knowing for sure. I didn't look in Ken's direction.

I didn't say much to anyone the rest of the day. Nobody did; Mr. Moore's words had weighed heavily on everybody's mind. And neither I nor anyone else went into Mr. Moore's office to report.

After school I cut out of the building alone, avoiding Anne and Stella, avoiding even Kenneth, which made me feel like a rat for I suspected he could have used my presence. I felt like a rat, too, for not stopping in to see how Celinda was feeling. But I was definitely not in the mood for a Browning Society discussion.

I went instead for a long walk on my own, up and down strange streets and eventually through the patch of woods. Involuntarily, as often happens to me in time of stress, I found myself writing poetry in my head. It was very abstract, for I didn't want to grapple with the realities of the situation. I wound up at last with a splitting headache and the realization that I was late for supper.

I went home to find the family already at the table and Mama too preoccupied with Pa to light into me. Pa was in that whimsical fatalistic mood of his, which means the roof is falling in but otherwise all is well.

". . . so anyway, she said I was accusing her of immorality, that her father would be in to punch me in the nose, that her parents would see that the school was put out of business because I was a dirty old man."

I slid hastily into my place at table and hissed, "What happened?" to Marnie who was sitting next to me.

"Viney came to school again in the peekaboo waist," Marnie whispered, "so Pa expelled her."

"Don't suppose," Mama said carefully, "there could have been some diplomatic way around it? So she wouldn't go out talking that way 'bout you?"

Pa looked at her. "Evie," he said quietly, "see-through clothes don't belong in a business office. They're distracting and bad taste. But that's not the moral issue. The real point is, I made a rule, and Viney knew it and she deliberately broke it. And if I transgress my own standards because I'm afraid of the consequences of abiding by them, then *I'm* immoral."

Pa's comment hit the spot, and the spot was sore. This was why, in all my wanderings, all my poetizing that afternoon, I had stayed in an equivocal condition. I had been passing judgment on the morality of Doug Latham and Mary Lou Hodge, instead of grappling with that of Letitia Chambers Sterling. For the cold hard fact, which I'd been ignoring just as I'd ignored the issue of my joining the Browning Society again, was that although I could not justify it, although I thought myself wrong, I was not going to report what I had seen to Mr. Moore.

And the ironic thing was that probably everybody in school would have agreed that I was right. Everybody but me. I knew perfectly well the reason for not telling, but that wasn't what held me back; I have nothing but respect for Kenneth, who on New Year's Day, and my father, who today, had transgressed that unwritten code.

No, what held me back was that I could not be sure of
purity of the reasons *for* my telling. That, and the fact that I
no longer had the stomach for the lonely role of crusader.

So Doug and Mary Lou will get away with their escapade.
And if, later, because they are not confronted with themselves
this time, they get into greater trouble, I may be in a way
responsible. But I will cross that bridge when I come to it. Not
now.

I do not like myself very much tonight.

CHAPTER THREE

January

It is revolting how fast one's sense of anticipation in getting back to school after vacation gets killed in the daily round. I will not go into the matter of how one's other sensibilities also get smothered. I get a bit tired of hearing how these are supposed to be the best years of our lives. Parents, obviously, have forgotten: Or else school has changed a lot since the Dark Ages. I notice Pa's not quite so glib in his pronouncements since he's been exposed to the harsh reality of classroom life.

Pa did kick Viney Hodge out, and there were repercussions. Mr. Hodge went storming down to the secretarial school, full of protective wrath over his poor innocent little girl, and implying that Pa was a dirty old man, but Pa stuck to his guns.

"Good thing he didn't come here to the house to speak his piece!" Mama snorted. "Have told him a few things he obviously doesn't know! Innocent little girl, my hat!"

Mama didn't feel so good, though, when she found out two of the other students had withdrawn from school as a result of the occurrence, or when she found out Mrs. Hodge was telling her own one-sided version at the Ladies' Aid.

"Let her say her piece. Whole neighborhood knows your Pa's reputation. *And* the Hodges'!" And despite the fact that her back was killing her, she made Pa a seven-layer cake for dessert.

That was on the Tuesday following the Browning Society debacle. On Wednesday Celinda came to school, recovered from her cold and the mysterious ailment, which she still fortunately did not understand. The sky was bleak, and before we left for home, snow was falling. "Come home with me," I said to Celinda. "Mama's made seven-layer cake."

Celinda looked torn. "Mama'll skin me. She thinks I'm out too often as it is."

"Rats," I said inelegantly. "I haven't seen you for ages. We can start working on our English projects, if that makes your conscience feel any better."

"Now there," Celinda said, "you have something."

So Celinda came over, and so did Anne and Stella, and I need not tell you we did not get much done on our English projects. By late afternoon the snow was coming down hard and the sky was the color of lead, and all the little kids in the neighborhood had dragged out their sleds and were in the process of getting soaked. Presently Pa came in, sleet frosting his hat brim above his tired eyes.

Stella jumped up. "Glory! I should have been home ages ago." Her tone was light but her eyes, as she said good-by to me, were searching. I suspected she had heard the rumors about Pa's run-in with the Hodges. There isn't much that gets past Stella.

Mama, too, had picked up the vibrations Pa had brought in with him. She hauled herself with effort off the sofa where she had been resting her aching back and started throwing dinner together, assisted by me and Marnie. But it wasn't till she had her Galloping Chicken on the table that she turned and faced Pa, hands on hips.

"Let's have it," she said. "What's the latest installment?"

Pa smiled ruefully. "Another young lady dropped out today. We are now down to half the original number of students."

"Hmph," Mama said. "Don't appreciate what they're getting, is all. Tide will turn. You'll see." And she dished Pa up an extra-big portion of Galloping Chicken, so named because one small fryer could gallop through portions enough for ten or more.

In the middle of all this the front door opened and who should walk in but Bron and Mr. Albright! From the tumultuous reception they received, you would have thought they'd been away a year.

"Land sakes! Weren't expecting you till the weekend! Set more places at the table. Must be frozen!" Mama was bustling around, thanking her stars there was enough chicken to go round. Mr. Albright was trying to disentangle himself from Cicero, who had felt called upon to offer an exceedingly slobbery welcome, and Bron pulled up a chair and started to laugh.

"It's kind of nice to know some things around here never change!"

Bronwyn looked radiant. She was wearing a new set of dark furs, boa and toque and muff. She had had her ears pierced and was wearing diamond earrings. As for Mr. Albright, I swear he looked ten years younger. Which is fine, since he's so much older than Bron anyway.

"Don't have to ask if marriage is agreeing with you two," Pa said drily. "But why in thunder did you come home early?"

"We read the weather reports. There's a blizzard on the way." Mr. Albright grinned. "Think Kate will mind having Sadie move in with her a few days early?"

Sourpuss Sadie had been staying on at the Albright house

to look after Junius, Mr. Albright's teen-age son, while his father was away. Mr. Albright went to the telephone to inform her they were home, and pretty soon Sadie and Junius and our Aunt Kate all walked in, and as you can well imagine my English assignment did not get much attention paid to it that night.

Mrs. Owens reminded us all of it in class the next afternoon. "A detailed thematic analysis of a book-length work of British fiction. At least ten pages' worth. It's due the end of the month, and for you procrastinators I had better point out that mid-year exams begin a week from today." That effectively scared us all, and so did the remembrance that Mr. Grimes's little project was also due very, very soon.

When I came out of the Girls' Cloakroom after school that afternoon, Kenneth was waiting for me. "I don't have to work today. Let's go to the Library and get started on those assignments."

That was decidedly a good idea, although I was finding it increasingly hard to concentrate on studies when Ken was around. He had better discipline than I did, however. After the usual amount of preliminary hushed talk and laughter, and being shushed by the librarian, who was indulgent because she knew us both, Ken went straight to the fiction shelf, browsed briefly, selected a book, and settled down to work. I infinitely prefer to do reports on books I have already read, and I'm not particularly enamoured of novels anyway, so I fiddled around, poking in this and that, and ended buried in my old favorite, *Idylls of the King*. Pretty soon I was happily back in the Land of Avalon, seeing Kenneth's face in place of Lancelot's, and wondering if I could persuade Mama to name the new baby Alisounde in place of whatever Pa dreamed up this time around.

Presently Kenneth put down his book, stretched, and looked

at the clock. "It's nearly five. Guess we'd better be starting home." His voice sounded dazed. "How about you, Tish? Did you find a topic?"

"What do you think of my chances for getting Mrs. Owens to consider *Idylls of the King* a book-length work of fiction? Ken? What's wrong?"

"Nothing's wrong," Ken said. But his voice still sounded odd. "It's this book. It's a corker. But it's strange. It's about this man whose portrait ages instead of him, and all the things that happen because his character never shows on his face." He held it out to me. It was by somebody named Oscar Wilde, and its title was *The Picture of Dorian Gray*. "In a weird kind of way," Kenneth said slowly, "it reminds me of my brother." He stood up, shook his head as if to clear it, and steered me to the check-out desk. The librarian turned a little pale when she saw the book he had.

"Are you *sure* that's the one you want?"

"Absolutely," Kenneth said. "Don't worry, Miss Vale. I won't pass it on to Tish."

Miss Vale looked disapproving. "Obviously," she said, "school has changed a lot since I was in it."

I thought Ken had been joking about not letting me read the book, but I found out later he wasn't. Part of me felt cherished and protected, and part of me wondered what the dickens was in that book that he didn't want me to see.

When I got home, Mama told me that Celinda had called. "Not five minutes ago. Wants to talk to you right away."

What on earth, I wondered, going to the phone. Celinda doesn't get to talk on the telephone too much, because her mother considers it a pernicious instrument that encourages the sin of gossip. But Celinda, when I reached her, wasn't wasting time on gossip. "I have to talk to you," she said without preamble. "Right away. Alone. Can you meet me at our place in the vacant lot?"

"At this hour? And it's starting to snow again."

"It will only take a minute. You've got to, Tish. Yes, Mama, I'm coming." And she hung up abruptly.

I informed my own mother of the inexplicable need for my immediate departure and took off for our childhood meeting place, a discarded drainage pipe in the park a few blocks away. Celinda had gotten there ahead of me, and her face was grim.

"Why didn't you tell me what it was made me sick at the Browning Society party?" she demanded.

"Who told you?" It was, I realized instantly, the wrong thing to say.

"Then it is true." Celinda's expression hardened. "Mama heard about it at the church meeting this afternoon. At least, she heard that 'some immoral heathen hooligans' had spiked the punch. She didn't put two and two together, thank God. But I did. Tish, how could you? Let me walk into school yesterday and face everybody, after I'd made a fool of myself like that, and not even know!"

"You stop right there," I said firmly. "You didn't make a fool of yourself. If anybody did, it's—well, never mind."

"Doug Latham, I'll bet you any money," Celinda interjected tartly.

I ignored that. "You'd been sick all that day, everybody knows that. Nobody's putting two and two together where you're concerned. Nobody knows about it except me and Ben. And Mrs. Owens. And I guarantee you we're not going to say a word." Then I remembered about Stella, but decided I'd better not mention that. "As for why I didn't tell you, if you must know, it's because I was afraid of your taking it exactly the way you have."

"I made a fool of myself," Celinda repeated doggedly.

"Oh, for Pete's sake, you didn't do anything! Not even get silly, the way Mary Lou does. You just acted dopey sick, which you already were. It's not such a big thing anyway. Nobody else'd be bothered by it, and neither would you if you weren't so blame prudish."

"Thanks a lot!" Celinda's navy-blue eyes got very dark and she was starting to shake, not entirely from the cold. I looked at her and pulled the reins on my impatience fast.

"Why on earth are we fighting? We're not mad at each other. Cee, it was nothing, believe me. Nobody noticed, and you don't have to worry." The one I really felt like fighting with was Mrs. Dodds. It's one thing to bring your kids up with no morals, the way Mrs. Hodge apparently has, but in my opinion Mrs. Dodds goes to the other extreme. I wondered whatever would happen to Celinda when, inevitably, she discovered she was a human being with, as Gramps would delicately put it, "aims and urges."

"Don't worry," I repeated, and pointed out that if Celinda didn't want to get chills and fever all over again, we'd better be getting on home, since neither of us had bothered with the formality of overshoes and the snow was coming down hard.

Snow continued falling all through the night, and it was up to our knees when we started out to school on Friday morning. The corridors in school became slippery with slush, and snowballs kept turning up in the most unlikely places. The little kids had a field day playing out of doors all weekend. By late on Saturday the snow had stopped, and around suppertime Kenneth telephoned.

"Some of the fellows have shoveled off the ice on the pond. Let's get the crowd together and go skating."

We did, and it was glorious. Skating with Ken, I discovered, was almost as good as dancing with him. Afterwards we all went back to Breidenbachs' and made fudge, including Marnie, who's been pushing her luck with Mama lately and gets to do most things along with the high school crowd. She didn't get to go to Grace Church Young People's on Sunday night, but that was because Mr. Derbyshire suffers from the vain delusion that if only high-school students are allowed we will act with more decorum. Bron, who only graduated from high school last June, is sort of advisor-chaperone, and when Ben and I arrived on Sunday evening we discovered that Mr. Albright had now been dragged in, too. Not too many kids showed up, because of the weather, so we ended up going over to Albrights' to make more fudge.

Bron pulled me aside. "Tish, how's Mama? When I was over Friday, she didn't look too good."

"You know Mama," I said. "Her back's killing her but she can't sit still. She's fidgeting around trying to get things done before Whatsitsname arrives."

"I know that restless energy; she always gets it. Remember what she was like before Missy came?" Bron's brow puckered. "That means the baby must be due very soon."

"Mama says another three weeks."

"Babies can't read calendars," Bron retorted. "Call me every day, will you, Tish, and keep me posted? You know it's no good my asking Mama how she feels."

By Tuesday Mama was jumping out of her skin, especially since Pa wouldn't let her leave the house for fear of falling on the ice. As a matter of fact, the rest of us had all we could do to keep our balance, and it was pretty funny watching people attempt to navigate the slippery uphill path to the school.

"Got to find that fool bassinette," Mama said that night.

"Haven't seen it since I let Missy use it for her dolls. Time enough, but might as well be ready." She rubbed her back and sat down, looking grey. "Could kick myself. Weren't caught in this trap, could be down helping your father with the school. Another baby all we need, land knows."

"I'll find the bassinette," I said. "Let me fix it up, will you, Mama? I saw a gorgeous picture in the *Ladies' Home Journal*."

"Ruffles and frills just for first babies," Mama said absently. "Too much work." But after dinner I took a lamp and went up to the attic, feeling secretly determined. Poor little unwanted Whatsitsname deserved *something* to welcome it.

I looked all over, but I couldn't find the bassinette anywhere. And land knows what condition it would be in after Missy had gotten finished with it. "I'll look for it right after school tomorrow," I promised myself.

When I came out of school on Wednesday, the sky was leaden and Kenneth was waiting for me. "Let's go back to the Library and get some more work done," he suggested. "We may not be able to again if the weather gets really bad." Already large white flakes were falling inexorably downward.

I'll look for the bassinette after dinner, I thought, and tucked my hand through the arm Ken offered me.

Predictably, we were in the Library a very long time, and when we emerged it was already dark. "And I forgot to telephone Mama! She'll about skin me!"

"Come on," Ken said, "I'll get you home." It was slow going, for the snow was high. A cold wind had risen, blowing the snow in icy sheets against our faces. Our feet, sinking through the drifts, struck yesterday's ice and we slipped and fell. We felt like Arctic explorers moving in slow motion, and unaccountably I was beginning to feel nervous.

"If this keeps up," Ken said, "there mayn't be school to-morrow." I gripped his arm hard. I didn't want to say anything, but I was getting scared. The whirling snow blotted out the gaslight, and I could barely recognize the familiar streets. Ken took my icy hand in his and squeezed it. "Almost there. Just one more block."

We passed my enterprising brother Peter, out shoveling neighbors' walks. He paused, leaning on the shovel handle, his breath coming in a frosty cloud. "Tell Ma that Ben and Marnie are out shoveling, too. They stopped and told me to tell her, but I haven't had time."

We plodded on through the storm. In the windows of the houses we passed, lamps emitted feeble ghostly glows. I buried my face in my muffler and clung to Kenneth's arm.

"Here's your house," Ken said. I lifted my face and felt a prick of fear.

"There's no lights on. That's queer."

"Maybe your mother's lying down." Ken knew how jittery I was getting these days about Mama. "Want me to come in with you?" he asked.

"No. You'd better get home yourself. Your mother will be worried." I said good-by and battled my way up the steps as he went off and was lost in the swirling snow.

Inside, everything was dark and still. "Mama?" I called, and then more sharply, *"Mama?"* but there was no reply. I ran, discarding outer clothes in a trail behind me, through all the silent house. Mama wasn't in the kitchen, in her bedroom, in the attic. I ran downstairs again, icy fingers closing around my backbone.

"Mama!" I yelled again, in real panic. I listened, straining my ears. And this time I detected a faint groan. It was barely more than a whisper, and it was frightening, but it was defi-

nitely Mama. I dashed back to the kichen and opened the cellar door.

"Mama? Is that you?"

"It's not the woodwork," Mama's weak voice said with asperity. "Come here, Tish. Quick."

I lit a lamp with trembling fingers and started down the cellar stairs, and there at their foot, in a little heap, lay Mama, gripping the stair pole hard. "Remembered I'd stashed that fool bassinette down here," she panted. "Somebody'd left a roller skate on the steps. Thank the Lord I didn't land on Whatsitsname. But I can't get myself up." For Mama to admit the need for help was the measure of her condition.

It may be a cliché to say my heart was in my throat, but at that moment it really was. I ran down and got my arm around Mama's nonexistent waist, and between the two of us, using the stair pole for leverage, we pulled her to her feet. Mama's back arched and her face twisted with pain. "Old fool . . . thought you'd never get home. . . ."

And all that time I'd been down at the Library, face it, not because of the work I was getting done but because of Kenneth's nearness. I hadn't even bothered to phone. I'd have kicked myself if it would have done any good. "I'm here now. Mama, do you think you can make it up the stairs?" Step by step, we made it, Mama's weight sagging heavily against me. I got her into the kitchen where she dropped down into the rocker and rubbed her back absently.

I put the kettle on, always the first revival measure in our house, and stared at her anxiously. "Are you all right? I'd better call Dr. Tuttle."

"Don't you dare!" Mama's eyes flew open. "Not dragging the poor man out on a night like this! 'Fraid you'll have to fix dinner, though. Where is everybody?"

"Missy's curled up asleep in the attic, the other kids are out shoveling snow. Pa may not get home; it's awful out. Mama, are you sure you're all right?"

"Don't sass me, young lady. I ought to know," Mama snapped. But I saw her wince again when she thought I wasn't looking. I slapped supper together, wishing fervently that the others were home. Presently they came drifting in, red-faced and frozen and breathing heavily, and Missy wandered down, attired rakishly in my best wrapper, a Roman sash, and pearls.

Marnie frowned. "It's funny we haven't heard from Pa," she said, and went to the telephone with determination. "I'm going to call the school." But after cranking vigorously several times, she turned away, looking puzzled. "The lines must be down. There's absolutely no sound at all."

"Pa probably tried to call us and couldn't get through." I saw Mama go through the wincing back-arching again, and she dragged herself to her feet. "Mama, sit down. I can get dinner on the table without your help."

"Not aiming to," Mama said, biting her lip. "Going up-stairs . . . lie down. Ben, you help. . . ." She reached a blind hand out to him, and he jumped up quickly, and Marnie and I exchanged worried looks.

When Ben came downstairs again he was looking grim. "I don't like the looks of it," he said bluntly. "I wonder if I ought to go try to get Doc Tuttle? Tish, Aunt K has a sign up in her window. I read it with the opera glasses. Pa called her when he couldn't get an answer here. He's not trying to come home."

"If he can't make it, neither can Doc Tuttle," Marnie said. "You'd better stay here where we don't have to worry about you, too."

By silent consent we didn't discuss the situation in front

of Peter and Missy, but as soon as supper was over, I dragged Ben and Marnie into the off-limits privacy of Pa's study and told them about Mama's fall. "Lord God," Marnie breathed. Her face was white. "If I left that skate there, I'll kill myself."

"Who did it's not important now," Ben said tersely. "I'll get the little guys to bed. You two had better stay with Ma." We didn't say what all of us were thinking: it was not good for a forty-year-old woman expecting a baby any day to take a fall like that.

Ben corralled the little kids, Marnie cleaned up from supper, and I went up to Mama. She was lying on the bed with her eyes closed, one hand rubbing her back. I sat down on the edge of the bed, and her face twisted.

"Mama?"

"I'm all right. Get kids to bed."

"Ben's doing that. Pa called Aunt Kate. He's not coming home." Mama's body arched suddenly, and her fingers grabbed hard at my wrist. "Mama, what is it?"

"Just a pain—will pass." Her fingers hung on to me a moment, then relaxed. There were little white lines around her lips, and she looked suddenly old. "Tish, go make me . . . cup of tea."

"I don't think I should leave you."

"*Git*," Mama snapped, and I decided I'd better do whatever she wanted. She was certainly in no shape to have a fight.

The wind was battering around the eaves and the house was chill. Ben went down cellar to stoke the furnace and returned with the bassinette. I made Mama's tea and took it up to her, followed by Marnie, who was looking kind of grey and scared. Mama was pacing up and down the room and rubbing the hollow of her back.

"Mama, for pity's sake, go back to bed."

"Can't stay put any more." Mama stopped and her lips flattened. ". . . time is it?"

"Ten to nine."

Mama took a gulp of tea, clattered the cup back into the saucer, and looked at Marnie. "Bed."

"Mama, don't be ridiculous. It's too early." Mama grabbed my wrist suddenly, and Marnie saw it. "And I'm certainly not going to leave you alone," Marnie said.

". . . what I say. No strength to fight. Mean it, Marianna." Mama took a deep breath, which steadied her somewhat. And Marnie looked at her face and came to the same conclusion I'd reached earlier, and went out silently. I started to follow, but Mama's fingers closed again like a vise around my arm.

"Wait. Close . . . door." Her lips formed the words soundlessly.

I obeyed, and when I turned back Mama was hanging on to the bedpost, her lips twisted into a rueful grin. "Oh, Lord. Hate to do this to you, Tish, but the baby's coming."

I stared at her.

"Fall must've started things moving," Mama said. "Won't be—couple of hours yet. Keep Marnie out. Bad enough . . . you be here. But you're oldest. Going to need you."

This was definitely not the moment to tell Mama I was scared out of my skin.

"Advantage to being seventh . . . know what to do." I could swear Mama sounded half-proud. "Baby blankets in hall closet. Warm them by grate. Better bring can of olive oil, and ball of twine."

I didn't want to leave Mama, but it was undoubtedly better now than later. In the hall I encountered Marnie hovering. "What's the matter?" she whispered. "I know darn well something is."

"The baby's started coming."

Marnie's jaw dropped. "You're joking."

"I wish I were. Go down and get the olive oil and twine for me, will you? Leave them outside the door."

"Now you are joking." Marnie saw my face, and her own set stubbornly. "I'm better than you are at this kind of mess, and you know it. And I know a heap sight more about birthing. You've been too squeamish to even watch the cats."

"I know it. But it's the way Mama wants it." I felt suddenly wobbly and tired. "Oh, Marnie, please don't fight. Help me!"

"All right, all right. But I still think it's crazy." Marnie went downstairs, and I went back to persuade Mama to go to bed.

"Absolutely not. One advantage . . . no doctor. Have things the way I want for once." So for the next hour, while the pains grew closer, Mama and I walked back and forth on a narrow strip of bedroom carpet, stopping occasionally when she caught her breath and her back arched. And in between I rubbed her back, and Mama talked about anything that came into her head. I had never felt closer to my mother in my life.

Marnie came back with the things that Mama'd ordered, and met me at the door. "Aunt Kate has another sign up. Wanted to know what was wrong. How do you suppose she can always tell? So I wrote back."

"You think she can read it?"

"With *her* spyglass? Maybe if her phone's not down she can get through to Pa or the doctor. Tish, I don't care what Mama says, if you need me, yell. I'll be right outside."

I went back, closing the door soundlessly behind me. Mama was hanging onto the bedpost. She had finally condescended to get undressed and was wearing a faded old wrapper. Another quarter of an hour went by . . . a half. . . .

The wind whistled crazily outside the windows, and snow flung itself against the panes in wild white sheets. It was like the night in November when Marnie and Missy had been so sick. But Bron had been with me then. Now I felt as if Mama and I were alone in a sleeping world. Mama wasn't pacing any longer; she alternately rested against the edge of the bed or clung to the bedpost. She wasn't talking any longer, either, and her face was grey. The pains were coming closer now, and harder; I could tell from the way Mama's fingernails dug into my wrists. Mama's an old woman, I thought in panic, looking at her face. God, if something goes wrong because I don't know what to do . . . oh, God, don't let her die.

"I think," Mama said faintly, "had better lie down." So I helped her onto the bed, and dipped a washcloth in cold water and bathed her face. Mama gasped, hard, and pressed her feet against the footboard, and bore down.

"Mama, for heaven's sake, go ahead and holler! You don't have to keep up a front with me!"

Mama was staring over my shoulder at the window, her tired eyes widened. "Must be seeing things," she murmured.

"It's the tree branches tapping." Then I heard it myself, louder than tree branches, and with it a sound like a human voice. I turned and, the state of my nerves being what they already were, I almost let out a screech to wake the dead. Outside the window, in the swirling snow, appeared the disembodied face of my Aunt Kate.

For a minute I stared, then I was running to the window, fumbling with the jammed catch, throwing it open. I grabbed Aunt Kate's arms and pulled her, wet and half-frozen, into the room.

"*Kate?*" came Mama's incredulous whisper. "How in tarnation?"

"Slid down the shed roof on my best tea tray," Aunt Kate said with satisfaction. "I can still steer, too, if I do say so. Straight into the old maple. Snow's high enough I could reach the big branch that interlocks with yours. Ed used to do that all the time when he was a boy. Figured it should be sturdy enough to hold me, too."

Mama was gazing at her dearest enemy with a mixture of emotions. "Kate Sterling, you're stubborn as an old coon. Didn't have to."

"Nonsense. Family. What do you take me for? It's all right, Tish. I'll take over now. You can go to bed."

"Tish stays," Mama said through gritted teeth.

Talk about mixed emotions, I was absolutely riddled with them. But I wasn't going to chicken out, not if I turned pea green, not with Mama wanting me.

It helped having Aunt Kate there. She could boss Mama better than I could. She tied a couple of towels to the bed-post for Mama to hang onto, looked Mama straight in the eye, and said, "Go ahead and yell if you've a mind to, Evie. You don't have to prove anything to me. I already know you've got grit." Which was, perhaps, the most surprising thing of that incredible night.

The pains were only a few minutes apart now, and Aunt Kate hovered, timing them on her father's old turnip watch. Mama was grimly concentrating on the job at hand. I sat on the edge of the bed and bathed Mama's face, and prayed with every fiber of my being. Oh God, please God, take care of Mama and don't let us make things worse.

Mama let out what was for her a screech, and her body lifted and contorted. Then she lay back, exhausted, on the pillows, and her head turned towards Aunt Kate wearily. "Think I'm an old fool, Kate, but know what I'd really like right now—" Her lips flattened with a spasm of pain, then went on. "Would you go downstairs, make me—one of your nice tart glasses of lemonade? . . . so hot in here. . . ."

Aunt Kate stood, torn between responsibility and importance. "Tish can do it. I don't like to leave you."

"No. You," Mama said strongly. "Children don't make it right like you do." That was a whopper if I'd ever heard one; Mama had frequently remarked that Aunt Kate's potations were as sour as her disposition. But Aunt Kate, of course, had never heard that. "Lemons in the cellar—Marnie can get them. Take your time—lots of time yet. *Please*, Kate."

That last appeal did it. Aunt Kate bustled out, flattered, after one last backward look. Mama's tired eyes turned to me with sheepish triumph. "Couldn't face having her here," she confessed. "Not fair—put you through this at your age—" Her lips flattened again and her back arched. "You can take it, can't you?"

My heart was pounding, and my insides were doing flip-flops, but I'd have died on a cross before I'd have admitted it to Mama, who'd chosen me, who was whispering, "Just keep your head—do exactly what I say—" She grabbed the bedposts and dug her heels into the mattress hard. "If you've got time—say a few fast prayers. . . ." Thank goodness Mama, after six kids, was an old pro. She muttered instructions through gritted teeth, and I didn't have a chance to feel scared or squeamish. And in another few minutes I was staring down into the decidedly angry face of my new sister. Only I didn't know she was a sister yet.

I cannot write it. I try, and something stops me, and it's not embarrassment. It was too private, and kind of sacred; private to Mama, and to me because she'd chosen me to share it with her. It was a blooming miracle, happening right there within my shaking hands.

Last summer at the farm, Peter had collected caterpillars,

which had promptly turned themselves into chrysalises like dried dead leaves. One dim gold afternoon I'd heard Peter calling, "My *citheronia regalis*'s going to hatch," and we had all gathered. It, too, had been a miracle. First nothing, then a tiny tear, then something unbelievably large and damp, half-propelled, half-pulling itself through that tiny hole. We watched, scarcely breathing. The *thing* finally lay there, wet and grotesque and somehow obscene. Then slowly, something stirred . . . the dampness dried, before our eyes wings grew and unfurled. My heart almost stopped with real pain at the wonder and the beauty of that moment. It was like that now. One more pulsing spasm and there she was in my hands, tiny and wet and red in her glistening transparent covering like angel's wings—unmistakably alive and human and fighting mad. I could even see the infinitesimal blue tracery of vein in her temple as she screwed up the energy for the mewing wail of an outraged kitten.

Behind me, Mama chuckled. "Sterling, all right. All my children ready to tackle the world from birth. Clean it off with olive oil, Tish, and give it here." She stretched and closed her eyes.

Already Whatsitsname was exhibiting the family trait of being uncooperative and was wailing her head off. She was so little and slippery and squirmy I was scared to death I'd drop her, so I deposited her hastily on the foot of the bed, still mewing. And then I did drop the bottle of oil and burst into tears, and in walked Aunt Kate, with the lemonade in her hand and a comical expression on her face, torn between relief and guilt that she'd missed it all. She took over with the baby, thank goodness, and I went over to the bed where Mama was holding out her hand to me.

"Good girl," Mama said tersely, and I started to cry again,

for that was as close as Mama could come to giving an accolade to somebody's face. But we didn't need words. Now that it was over, the exhaustion showed and she looked her age. I bathed her face and started trying to clean up the mess. Mama's eyes followed me. "Sorry you had to see it," she said. "Not right. Too young."

"I'm not sorry," I said softly. "It was beautiful. Mama, I—I'll never be afraid now."

"One thing I'm good at's having babies," Mama said complacently. "Easy as shelling peas. It's carrying them aforehand gets me down. By the way, what is it?"

"A girl. She's got Bronwyn's dark hair, and it sounds like Marnie's temper."

"Oh, Lordy!" Mama said fervently. She took a sip of the lemonade and made a face. "Tish, *you* drink it—or throw it out—or something. I'd have another baby right now before I'd drink that sour stuff." I swallowed it hastily, and then Aunt Kate came in with Whatsitsname all cuddled up in a warmed blanket and looking like a sleepy kitten, and put her in the bassinette Marnie had quickly trimmed. We sponged Mama off and helped her into a fresh nightgown, and I combed and rebraided her damp hair, and then we transferred her across the hall to my room, where Marnie had hurriedly made up the bed with the best embroidered sheets scented with lavender. Mama insisted on walking down the hall herself, proving that stoicism does have its advantages, but she looked kind of wilted afterwards and was glad to get resettled.

The baby began mewing again with indignation, and Marnie and I wheeled the bassinette in carefully, and Mama took the little white wooly bundle up with her. There was a clattering beyond the door, and Ben called, "I can't hold the little kids back much more. Missy's determined to see the baby," and Mama said resignedly, "No privacy in this house nohow, all right, let them in." Peter, as became a budding scientist, inspected the baby carefully from a distance, but Missy was fascinated. She breathed a delighted, "Oo-ooh!" and climbed up on the bed, and had to be held back by the hem of her nightie.

It occurred to me that the only times I'd ever seen Mama serene and relaxed and not boiling over with restless energy was when she was nursing her babies. She traced the blue vein in Whatsitsname's temple gently with one finger, and the baby's hand, flailing aimlessly, encountered Mama's. The tiny pink curves, with their unbelievable little fingernails, closed by instinct around her finger. "See that?" Mama said tenderly. "Knows how to do that without being taught. Happens automatically."

Something else happened automatically in our family, I thought, my eyes roving around the room warm with lamplight while outside the window the snow still fell in the silent blackness. I had wasted so much time the past months, worrying about poor little Whatsitsname arriving unwanted and unloved. I hadn't needed to worry at all.

"Can't go on calling her Whatsitsname," Mama said. "Not polite." She looked at me. "You've earned the right. *You* name it."

"You're taking a big chance," Marnie said darkly. "What kind of goopy stuff has Tish been reading lately, the Middle Ages or those ancient Greeks?"

I shot her a baleful look, and behind her shoulder I saw Aunt Kate hovering in the doorway, having come from the unlovely job of cleaning up the delivery room, and hesitant about intruding into our tight little family circle. She was back to being her dour, gloomy self. But superimposed on that image, as in one of Mr. Albright's trick photographs, I saw others. The ludicrous sight of Aunt Kate's face outside the window as she crawled along that precarious tree branch to reach us. Aunt Kate standing in the doorway with her little satchel the night the girls got the fever. Aunt Kate and Bron and me working side by side during the midnight hours when Marnie almost died. Aunt Kate a few hours ago gripping Mama's hand and saying, "Go ahead and yell if you've a mind to, Evie. You don't have to prove anything to *me*."

"Well?" Mama said. "Never thought it'd take you this long, Tish. What's the name to be?"

"Katherine," I said. "She's Katherine Allison."

CHAPTER FOUR

February

My head throbs; I wish that I could sleep. But my brain won't rest, my mind is teeming with unanswerable questions.

Pa would say that's just like me, trying to solve the riddles of the universe before I'm fifteen. But I don't give two hoots about the Greeks and their imponderable enigmas, I just want some simple answers I can give to Celinda now. Or maybe I need them to convince myself.

Why does God let some things happen? Because if God *is* God, He shouldn't. I don't mean I'm mad at God exactly, but I'm fed to the teeth with church, and religion, and being religious, and the bad things people can do in its name. And I'm sore as hell at people who keep all the commandments except the law of love. So here I sit at a quarter to noon on a Sunday morning, staring out my window at a wan February landscape and trying to figure out what I can believe.

It seems an age since the baby was born. A few days later the sun came out and the snow thawed enough for both Pa and Dr. Tuttle to come battling through the snowdrifts, both of them considerably surprised to find Katherine Allison here before them. Mama was back on her feet sooner than anyone expected, so by Katie's one-week birthday, Aunt Kate was back in her own home, to everyone's relief. Gratitude can be a pretty wearing thing to have to live with.

Katie's a good baby, who seldom even cries, and Bron comes up every day to help Mama, so soon life settled back pretty much into our old routine. What with Christmas and Katie's imminent arrival, I had gotten pretty much behind in my work at school, and several teachers had rather caustic comments to make when they returned mid-year exams. Classes grew harder; teachers, sighting a long uninterrupted stretch of time before spring vacation, piled on the work. The days were enlivened by the usual wintertime diversions—an unexpected fire drill during a sleet storm, courtesy of Doug's accepting Ben's dare to pull a false alarm; snowball fights in the hall with ammunition scraped from window ledges.

It was around this time, too, that some rowdies discovered another sport. Our first inkling of it came as we were leaving school on Monday afternoon. The teachers, as usual, were urging us to leave and do our socializing at home instead of in the corridors, and I was stalling, trying to find out whether Ben had reported for the detention he'd been assigned for putting a snowball on the seat of his math teacher's chair. Finally Sourpuss Sadie grabbed Celinda and me by the shoulders and steered us firmly towards the stairs.

"I've heard all I care to for one day about that dance your sister's dreamed up. I don't see what a church has to be holding a dance for, anyway."

The dance she meant was the one Bron had persuaded Mr. Albright to talk Mr. Derbyshire into letting us have in the Parish Hall for Valentine's Day. Celinda hadn't been to Young People's the night before because her mother had dragged her to a revival meeting at her own church, and the notes we'd managed to exchange in classes had not done justice to the magnificence of the entire idea. I was determined Celinda was going to attend the dance, and it was going to be a job and a half to pull *that* off.

Celinda was her usual pessimistic self. "Mama's stricter than ever now. You should have heard the preacher last night!" She shuddered. Celinda's imagination always works overtime after revival meetings. I could understand it; I'd gone with her once and had nightmares three nights straight afterwards. Mama had put her foot down and said never again.

"What was it about last night?"

"Punishment for sin, and what would happen if the world ended tomorrow and we hadn't had a chance to repent." Celinda's eyes were troubled. She's torn more than she'll admit between the fire and brimstone of her mother's teachings and the love she hears about when she comes with me to Grace Church. "Mama brought home three whole boxes of tracts. She wants me to go around with her from door to door." The very thought had her in agony.

"Don't go home," I said sensibly. "Mama's making Stretchable Stew. Come stay for supper, and by the time you get home it'll be too late to go out."

We emerged into the grey dampness of a February afternoon. For once the younger boys who hang around weren't throwing snowballs at departing girls. They were dancing instead around a gaunt black figure on the corner. Beside me I heard Celinda groan, "Oh, no!" Sure enough, it was Mrs. Dodds. She was standing on the corner, attempting to hand out tracts to a group of jeering little monsters.

I grabbed Celinda's arm. "Cut back through the school and go out the other door. Then you can get over to our house without getting caught."

Celinda looked tempted. Just then a snowball started flying, and I knew exactly what Celinda would do. She went plowing into the fray, shamed but angry, and attempted to steer her mother home. Mrs. Dodds stood resolutely, her black cloak flapping in the wind, and I could hear something about "not afraid of persecution." A snowball knocked her glasses askew and another hit Celinda on the temple. Then behind me, blessedly, I heard, "All right, you guys, break it up!"

Ben and Doug had emerged from their incarceration, and Doug, despite his reputation, can be a good influence when he chooses. Within minutes the two of them had sent the smaller boys packing, and Celinda steered her mother off, and Ben and I went home.

"What was that all about?" Ben demanded.

"Mrs. Dodds was trying to hand out tracts."

Ben grinned. "Something tells me she isn't going to get far around here!"

After that, with increasing frequency, Mrs. Dodds would be out on the playground corner in the afternoons, waiting to hand out tracts to unwary children. She got to be a fixture there, a tall, rather pathetic and bedraggled black crow. It was very funny to everyone but Celinda.

It did not take long for the boys to discover that those tracts made lovely airplanes, and after that you were apt to find messages about fire and brimstone glaring down at you from the most ungodly places, like ceiling light fixtures or ventilator grilles. Pretty soon the principal had to send out a notice on the subject.

Meanwhile, plans for the Valentine's Dance were progressing. It was, in fact, becoming the talk of the school and was providing excellent publicity for Grace Church Young People's. You wouldn't believe how many new faces were present

Sunday night, seeking to get themselves put down as members so they'd be able to attend. Even Doug, who usually comes only when refreshments are offered, was there. Bron had talked Mr. Albright into persuading the Vestry to pay for having Mamie Wilcox play the piano for the dance. Mr. Albright convinced them the dance was their contribution towards Keeping the Kids of Yonkers Off the Streets.

To me, Bron confided the real reason she was knocking herself out so on the dance. "I'm determined I'm going to push that Junius out of his shell if I kill us both trying! Honestly, he's worse than Celinda!" Her shoulders sagged. "I never saw a boy his size so scared of his shadow! He turns tomato-colored every time he has to speak to me, and the words stick in his throat like peanut butter. All he's interested in is his bug collection!"

"Peter's just as bad."

"Yes, but Peter's years younger," Bron retorted. "He just couldn't be a loner, growing up in a family like ours. But poor old Junius! What can you expect when he's been living with Miss Albright for five years?" Bron still couldn't get used to having Sourpuss Sadie as a sister-in-law.

Bron's earlier words had given me an idea. "Maybe we could fix Junius up with Celinda! They couldn't possibly be afraid of each other."

Bron's eyes narrowed. "It just might work. Celinda's a sucker for an underdog, and she couldn't frighten a fly. You tackle her, and I," she murmured grimly, "will handle Junius."

Which explains why I had Celinda over to the house the next afternoon. The kitchen is really the heart of our home on bleak winter days. The teakettle bubbled cheerfully on the range. Mama had a nut cake in the oven; she was stirring up icing with one arm and holding Katie with the other. The center table was a cheerful mishmash of cooking things, mittens, and schoolbooks, with Ben and Marnie gathered around it doing homework. Celinda and I were making candy and discussing the dance. I was artfully painting a glowing picture of its glories, and I had just detected a wistful look in Celinda's eyes, when the kitchen door burst open.

"Mama! *Ma-a-a-ma-a-a!*" Missy, tearful and screeching, catapulted into the room and clutched at Mama's skirts for dear life. Mama, who knows a crisis when she sees one, handed Katie to me quickly.

"Land sakes, child, what's the matter? What's wrong?"

"That darn ol' Mrs. Dodds!" Peter said, banging the door shut behind him. He didn't notice, or didn't care, that Celinda was there. "That darn ol' crow! She told Missy that she was a sinner and that God was going to turn her into a little bird for punishment and she'd have to fly away and never see her folks again!"

"I don't wanna goooo!" wailed Missy, hiding her face against Mama's legs.

I saw Mama's eyes shoot sparks, but she glanced towards Celinda and only pressed her lips together in a thin straight line.

Celinda stood up, looking pale. "I'd better go home."

"Cee, wait! We haven't finished about the dance. . . ."

"Not now. I've got to find Mama. She's got to realize she can't do things like this." Celinda pulled her coat and scarf on and went out like a scared, determined little soldier.

It didn't look as if I was going to have much luck with Celinda about the dance. It didn't seem as if Celinda would make much progress with her mother, either, for Mrs. Dodds was back outside the high school the next afternoon, and the next. One day she even marched right into the school building and started buttonholing kids in the corridors, telling them of their need to be saved from the lake of everlasting fire. Celinda wasn't around at the time, thank goodness, and neither was Mr. Moore, which explained how Mrs. Dodds was able to be doing it in the first place. It was nearly five p.m. of a grey, sleety afternoon, and a goodly bunch of us had been hanging around discussing literature and life after a Browning Society meeting. The janitor, who'd been lurking outside Mrs. Owens's room for some time, had finally marched in and begun banging scrap baskets ostentatiously, and we'd decided that we'd better leave. We'd drifted downstairs in dribs and drabs after adjournment to the cloakrooms for our wraps, and there in the lower hall was Mrs. Dodds, with her hands full of shortcuts to salvation.

Behind me I heard Mrs. Owens murmur, "Oh, dear," and Mary Lou, predictably, giggled. I do not deny that Mary Lou could decidedly benefit from some salvation, but today Mrs. Dodds zeroed in on the boys instead. She got hold of Kenneth, who was too polite to duck. Coward that I was, I pulled the collar of Bron's hand-me-down coat up around my face, skirted the two of them widely, and just cut out. The raw sleet struck at me as I emerged, and I started down the hill alone, beginning to feel ashamed of myself. Celinda would have died of embarrassment if she'd been there, but she wouldn't have chickened out.

Besides, a little demon of selfishness whispered in my ear that if I'd stayed I might have been walking home with Kenneth instead of by myself.

I decided to stop by Albrights' on my way home, in search of hot cocoa and some self-esteem. Bronwyn could usually be counted on for both, and the hot nut bread she was taking from the oven when I arrived didn't hurt me either. Bronwyn listened to my tale of woe grimly. She had already, it developed, heard about Missy and the little bird from Mama. "There isn't much anyone can do about Mrs. Dodds standing outside, it's a public street. But coming into the school building may be different. I'll tell Sidney." Bronwyn had infinite faith in Mr. Albright's skill and wisdom. She refilled our cocoa cups, sat down across the table, and looked at me shrewdly. "There's something else bothering you, too, isn't there?"

I pushed the crumbs from my third piece of nut bread around my plate slowly. "Don't laugh, but when I walked out of there today I felt as if I were hearing the cock crow."

" 'Thou shalt deny me three times'?" Bron nodded. "People like Mrs. Dodds at least have the courage to practice their convictions, which, as Ben was pointing out a few months back, is something the rest of us fall down on all too often." She laughed ruefully. "Isn't it too bad the fanatics always seem to bring out the most *un*christian streak in the rest of us!" The front door creaked, and we looked up to see Junius slithering cautiously past the kitchen door.

"Junius! Come have some hot bread and cocoa!" Bronwyn called. Her voice was warm, but something in her tone put the brakes on Junius. He turned red and sidled into the kitchen, clutching his coat around him. The notion of his being Bronwyn's stepson still struck me as ludicrous, and I wondered if the rest of him was ever going to catch up with his height and ears. He nodded at me, avoided looking at Bronwyn, and sat down on the edge of the chair she hospitably pulled out. I had an idea Junius was proving a bit more than Bron had bargained for. "For goodness sake," Bron said irritably, at last, "take off your coat and stay a while."

Junius pulled the coat even tighter together. To our astonishment, the coat gave forth a tiny but very definite wail of protest. It was a toss-up whose face was more of a study, his or mine. But Bronwyn, after a baffled second, suddenly sounded very much like a mother indeed. "Junius Albright, what sort of animal have you got stashed in there? Get it out directly!"

I actually felt sorry for poor old Junius, who looked, himself, like an animal caught in a trap. He reached into his coat front, hauled out a protesting scrap of fluff that looked for all the world like a dirty drowned caterpillar, and deposited it on Bron's clean tablecloth. The little thing arched its back valiantly, spat, and shivered. It was without a doubt the tiniest, dirtiest kitten I had ever seen.

"Oh, the poor little thing!" Bronwyn swept down on it like Motherhood Incarnate, and the kitten blinked at her with enormous sapphire eyes. "Junius, get some hot water and the laundry soap, we'll have to give it a bath. Tish, run up to the linen closet and find some old towels. Get a lot so we can make a bed for it under the stove. And oh, Junius, see if you can find an old medicine dropper. It's too little yet to drink from a saucer."

Junius gaped at her. "You mean—you're going to let me keep it?"

"Junius Albright, don't you know me yet at all? You certainly didn't think I'd throw it out in the storm!"

Junius mumbled something to the effect that Aunt Sadie would have. "I'm not your Aunt Sadie," Bron retorted with spirit.

Junius looked as if he'd just awakened to discover it was Christmas. He was so happy he was actually goaded into speech. The burden of his message was that well, gee, er, if there was ever anything he could do for Bronwyn. . . .

Bronwyn's eyes narrowed in a manner I well knew. "Maybe there is," she murmured calculatingly. And that explains why

I received a phone call from my elder sister after dinner that night, informing me that Junius had agreed to ask Celinda to the Valentine's Dance.

"Fine," I said grimly. "Now how do I get Celinda to agree?"

"That's your department. I've done my part of the job," Bron said smugly. "Me and Aphrodite."

"Aphrodite?"

"The kitten. Oh, Tish, wait till you see how she's cleaned up! She has four white feet and the most beautiful tiger markings. Even Sidney adores her. Sidney's a real cat person."

I was in no mood for Bronwyn's rhapsodies of love. I hung up on her and concentrated on the problem of Celinda.

The best prospect seemed to lie in persuading Celinda that going with Junius would be an act of Christian charity towards Bronwyn. Accordingly, I favored Celinda with a somewhat magnified version of the kitten episode when we went to the Library the following afternoon. Supposedly we were doing research for another of Mr. Grimes's famous history papers, but our favorite niche was conducive to private gossip sessions. I embellished the tale with artistic details designed to prove that Junius was destined to real freak-of-nature status if he was not saved soon.

"He's a real animal nut." Celinda giggled. "You should have seen him in zoology class the day we cut up the frogs! He was as green as I was, only Junius was feeling sorry for the frog!"

"Bron says he's on the way to becoming one of those weird characters, like you read about in books, that can't talk to people at all. You know what he's like in a class when he has to recite! She thinks the kids are real rats to laugh at him instead of helping him get over being shy."

I played variations on this theme for the rest of the afternoon until I decided that between missionary fervor and guilt over noninvolvement, I'd given Celinda's Puritan conscience enough to think about.

There was a meeting of the decorations commitee for the Valentine's Dance at Bron's that night. Celinda didn't get to come—she's almost never allowed out on school nights—but the rest of our crowd was out in force. Under cover of helping her with refreshments, Bron pulled me into the kitchen. "Junius promised to invite her during school tomorrow. For goodness sake, come over in the afternoon and tell me what happens!"

I tell you, the next day in school was as good as a play—or would have been if I hadn't had my fingers crossed so hard. It took Junius all morning to pluck up courage to approach Celinda; it took her another hour before she got the nerve to let him say a word. Such blushings, such mumblings, such awkward maneuvers. The rest of the crowd soon tumbled to what Junius was leading up to, though they knew nothing of the machinations behind it, and they found the whole thing hysterically amusing, which made me furious. By the time we scattered for our last class of the day, I'd about given up hope, but Cee and Junius must have found something reassuring in their mutual antipathy towards dissections, for as soon as the three o'clock bell rang I saw Celinda hurrying towards me from the zoology classroom, looking pale. She pulled me with her into the Girls' Cloakroom. Her hands, I noticed, were actually trembling.

"Junius went and asked me to the dance on Saturday. The teacher made us be lab partners today, so I was trapped. Tish, what'll I do?"

"Say yes, you idiot," I hissed, glaring over Celinda's shoulder at Mary Lou, who was eavesdropping avidly.

"You know Mama'd kill me if I ever asked to go to a dance! She'd never let me near anything at your church again, ever, either!"

"Ask if you can stay overnight with me on Saturday. Then you'll have to go with me whatever I do, that's plain good manners." I steered Celinda firmly to where Junius was lurking outside the cloakroom door, and went off to give Bronwyn a victory report.

This affair of weight being settled, we were all free to concentrate on an event of greater import, namely the end of the marking period, which was rapidly approaching. We toiled and groaned and burned the midnight oil, and all tests were over and essay papers completed by the time Saturday dawned grim and lowering and overhung with sleet.

Despite the weather, the crowd that assembled to decorate the Parish House was in a slapstick mood. Even the older kids condescended to stop by, inspired no doubt by the fact that Bronwyn was supplying lunch. The presence of Ben, Doug, and their cohorts moved Mary Lou to even greater efforts than usual in the man-chasing line, and Stella started giving her competition for pure deviltry. Doug pinned a heart inscribed with a ribald message to the back of Mary Lou's skirt, and the good hour before she found out afforded the spectators infinite amusement. Bron and Mr. Albright brought us down soup and sandwiches and stayed to help, and by the time we dispersed at five to eat and dress, the place really did look nice.

Celinda appeared at the house in time for supper, lugging her suitcase and looking scared to death. "I've got a headache. I think I'm going to be sick. Maybe I shouldn't. . . ."

"Oh, no, you don't," I said brutally, shoving her into a dining room chair, and Mama, who was in on the plot, plunked a plate of Stretchable Stew down under her nose. For some reason Celinda always likes our groceries better than those at home, and presently she began to look less green. Afterwards, accompanied by Mama and Marnie, we hustled upstairs to get dressed, while Ben, who had already completed his preparations by putting on a clean shirt and a tie, went out on the porch to sneak a smoke, watch the storm, and wait for the boys' arrival. Mama's not so modern that she'll let me go to an evening party with a boy without a big brother being along; as a matter of fact I think she figures I put an effective damper on Ben as well, and she's probably not far wrong. Ben doesn't mind overmuch since he doesn't have a girl and he can't tag along with Doug and Mary Lou, whose parents don't give two whoops what they do and who emphatically don't want a third party along. By the time I'd been buttoned into my coral merino, and Celinda into her blue, we heard Ken and Junius come stamping up the porch steps.

The storm had subsided now to only a few sparse whirling crystals, but Vyse Avenue was a world of white. Long fingers of transparent ice sheathed the bare tree branches. The gas flames of the street lights caused them to give off a thousand rainbow fragments with which the wan moonlight, poking through the clouds, tried vainly to compete. Huddled and muffled against the wind, we all hurried downhill to the warmth and cheer and gaiety of the Parish House.

As usual at mixed crowd parties, it took a little while to get things going, but after a few circle games and Mamie's rendition of ragtime, the dance really took off. At first Celinda displayed all the social graces of a wet dishrag, but even she couldn't hold out for long. Mama must have had a little kitchen conversation with Ben, because he cut in on Junius somewhere around the third dance, and Kenneth of course didn't need any coaching to be polite, and after a while Celinda and Junius both looked enough alive that I didn't have to feel guilty about forgetting them and concentrating on having my own very good time.

The Vestry had insisted on party games as well as just dancing, and these were silly enough to break down anyone's resistance. They were followed by a break for punch and cake, and then the dances resumed, dreamier ones this time. I closed my eyes and gave myself up to the bliss of circling in Kenneth's arms, glad that Ben had apparently sneaked out for a smoke and therefore would not be apt to give Mama a too-accurate report. Then all at once Kenneth missed a step and exclaimed. "Well, for gosh sake!" in a tone so sincerely startled that I jumped.

"What? Where?" My eyes flew open, and there in the doorway was Mrs. Dodds. One moment she was standing there like a gaunt black crow, the next she was over where Celinda was standing.

Everything seemed in slow motion, as if under water. All conversation, all dancing in the circle around Celinda and her mother had ceased, and to my eternal shame we just stood transfixed. If we'd only had our wits about us, we might have saved Celinda, but we merely watched, like rabbits hypnotized by light, as Mrs. Dodds grabbed Celinda by the arm, forcing her to her knees.

"Slut . . . whore . . . vile abominations . . . evil lusts of the flesh . . ." I had never realized words straight from the Bible could sound so obscene. They struck at Celinda the way her mother's hand struck across her face, with deliberate repetition. Her mother's wedding ring left a red welt across her cheekbone, but Celinda just took it, unmoving, like a dumb beast awaiting slaughter.

It must have lasted all of sixty seconds. It seemed forever. Then Bronwyn was there, with Mr. Albright, looking as stern as an Old Testament patriarch, looming at her shoulder.

"Mrs. Dodds, I think we may take it from this that Celinda did not have your permission to attend this dance. We are sorry if you've been upset. But I am sure you would prefer to carry on your family discussion in your own home."

Bronwyn's eyes were like volcanos, but her voice was as icily polite as our Aunt Kate, and Mr. Albright added incisively, "You are entitled to your own beliefs, Mrs. Dodds, but this is a church party being held in our house of worship; we cannot have you blaspheming it with such irresponsible charges." His hand on her elbow, he steered her firmly toward the door.

Junius Albright, that lily-livered coward, had disappeared into the crowd, his face scarlet, so it was Ken and I who went to help Celinda to her feet. But Bronwyn's regality seemed to have pumped some starch into Celinda's spine. "Thank you, Tish . . . Kenny. I'm all right." Celinda's voice quivered, then steadied. Her head high, she followed her mother across the room with such dignity that we didn't dare go after.

I looked at Ken and he looked at me, and I thought I was going to be sick. "Tish Sterling, don't you dare!" Bronwyn had seen my face, and her fingernails dug sharply into my arm. "Get out there and start dancing," she hissed at us, "quick!" She ran across to the piano, and a few seconds later Mamie was banging out a polka. Shortly thereafter Mr. Albright, having returned from the cloakroom, was announcing a circle dance. He and Bron led it off. He'd probably never had to cope with a kids' party before, let alone a mess like this, but he was doing just fine. And I had a feeling that Junius was going to hear a few words from *pater familias* when we all reached home.

Home . . . my body kept bouncing through what was left of the evening as gaily as everyone else around me, but a lead weight was jouncing, too, in the emptiness that was my stomach. What was happening to Celinda in the holy crow's nest? I looked at Ken. "She'll be all right," Ken said. "Her mother must love her or she wouldn't act this way." But I didn't think he was any more sure of it than I was.

At eleven o'clock the party was over, and for once there didn't seem to be much difficulty persuading everyone to get the message. Apparently Mrs. Dodds's performance had put more of a damper on people than I'd realized. Bronwyn had planned to make Welsh rarebit for Ben, Ken and me, Celinda and Junius, but she didn't mention it now. There was a purposeful look in Mr. Albright's eye as he headed for Junius, who was hiding out, so Kenneth told me, in the Gents' Cloakroom.

"He got a look in the mirror at the Chicken of the Year and didn't like it," was Ken's terse summation of Junius's performance.

We walked up the hill through the chill bleak night in silence, Ken, Ben, and I. By some kind of mutual instinct we didn't even hold hands, climbing through the drifts. Drat and blast Mrs. Dodds, I thought violently to myself.

"I'll stop by to walk you to church," Ken said, when we reached the house.

"Yes, do," I said. I wished somehow that I could go to church right then.

Pa and Mama were still up, Pa with his nose in his endless bookkeeping, and Mama darning in the rocker close by. The lamp with its rosy shade cast a soft halo around her hair. "Awful. Ask Ben to tell you," I mumbled to Mama's query of how the dance had been, and headed for the stairs. I undressed in the dark and pulled three layers of blankets up to my chin, wishing Bronwyn were back in bed beside me.

I hadn't thought I'd be able to sleep, but I must have, for the next thing I knew was a jarring, faraway sound of the telephone shrilling insistently through the blackness. It took a few seconds for it to percolate through my fuzzy mind that I was probably the only one awake, then I was running downstairs barefoot through the night-cold house. I picked up the receiver groggily, then straightened, galvanized wide awake.

"*Celinda?* Cee, stop crying, and slow down, I can't understand you."

"I can't. I'll get caught." Celinda's whisper came in rushed spurts between lurching sobs. "I had to wait till I was sure she was asleep. Tish, you've got to help me. I can't stay here. Meet me at our place in the park."

"Cee, don't be crazy. You can't go there in the middle of the night, in February! Come to the house. . . ." I broke off, for Celinda had hung up.

"Who's that at this fool hour?" It was Mama's voice behind my shoulder, and I jumped.

"I'm sorry. I didn't want to wake you."

"Be up in half an hour anyway, with the baby," Mama said. "That Celinda?"

I nodded. "She's running away. She told me to meet her in the park, and then hung up."

"Bring her here, acourse." Mama's eyes were stern with compassion. "Ben told me. Get him to go with you; park's no place for either of you at this hour."

"I can't wait. I'm afraid of what she'll do if she gets there first and doesn't find me." I flung my coat on and jammed my feet into a pair of boots—in our house, fortunately, there's always a pile of assorted footgear near the kitchen door.

The night wind struck my face as I ran down the street, and the crack of ice beneath my feet resounded in the stillness. In point of fact I wasn't feeling anywhere near as unafraid as I'd tried to convey to Mama when I'd left the house. I wished fervently that I hadn't been reading so much Edgar Allan Poe lately, as I started diagonally through the frozen silence of the park. I ran so fast that my breath became a rasping knife in my throat, but fast as I was, I still found Celinda in the drainage tunnel before me. She was huddled in the snowy corner, on her knees, bent double like a wounded animal, and it was quite a while before I could get her to even speak.

"Celinda, what happened?" I could feel her shivering, even through her heavy coat, as I held her. "Tell me. You'll feel better."

Celinda shook her head. "More what you heard . . . at the dance. Don't make me say it." She shuddered. "I feel so dirty."

I stood up, pulling Celinda to her feet. "Come on," I said firmly, "we're going home."

Celinda shrank away. "I can't. Your parents—they'll make me go back. . . ."

"No, they won't. Mama's up, she knows, and she's feeling Aunt-Kate-ish." I got a good look at Celinda and felt cold in a way that had nothing whatever to do with the weather. "Cee, while you're alone, tell me. You know you have to. What did your mother do?"

In answer, Celinda's hands went stiffly up to untie her woollen scarf. A thin ray of moonlight aureoled her head. I caught my breath.

"Celinda, your *hair!*" It was chopped off, jaggedly, somewhere around her ears.

"She cut my fingernails, too," Celinda said dully. They were cut to the quick, and there was a thin trickle of blood on the finger that wore the little forget-me-not ring.

"Celinda, *why?*"

"To stop my sinful vanity," Celinda's voice said. "So no-body'd respond to my vile lusts of the flesh."

"I don't think," I said evenly, when I was able to speak,

"that you'll have to worry about my folks sending you home."

I got Celinda home with me by sheer Sterling stubbornness, but by the time we reached our corner she was docile with exhaustion. Lights streamed from the kitchen to welcome us. Pa was up, having pulled his trousers on over his nightshirt, "in case I had to come out after you," he said.

Ben and Marnie were up, too, but they faded tactfully into the background after one look at Celinda's face. The coffeepot was boiling. Mama was nursing Katie; she held the baby with one arm and poured coffee all round with the other. I got Celinda into a chair by the fire, and got her coat off and dried her feet, and after she had a cup of Pa's strong coffee, liberally dosed with milk and sugar, she began to look a little less like a corpse.

Pa sat down in the chair on the other side of the fire and lit his pipe. "Now," he said quietly, in the tone we kids knew well, "suppose you tell us what this is all about."

Cee didn't want to talk, but she couldn't hold out against Pa any more than I could. Bit by bit, it all came out, the horror intensified by the matter-of-factness of Celinda's little voice.

I can't write it down. Half of it my mind blotted out because I couldn't bear it; the other half I only wish I could forget.

Behind me I heard Ben mutter, "If the old crow always thought the lusts of the flesh were so vile, I wonder how Celinda ever got born." I jabbed an elbow into his ribs sharply, and he subsided. When Celinda was finished, the kitchen was very still.

Pa struck a match and relit his pipe, which had gone out. He looked at Celinda, sitting there like a limp rag doll with her chopped-off hair and reddish-purple smudges around her shuttered eyes. "Celinda," he said finally, "I'm going to make a speech I've got no business making, first because you're not my child, and second because I have no right to contradict your family's religious teaching. But I'm going to say it all the same."

His voice kindled. "Don't you ever be ashamed of being human, Celinda, and don't ever let anyone make you ashamed of wanting to be a real woman. Or ashamed of the human body and its feelings, either, because it was made by God, and I don't reckon anything God gives us can be dirty. If you use it irresponsibly, then yes, that's cheapening something God made to be beautiful and sacred. But the wanting that happens between a man and a woman when they truly love each other and are ready to belong to each other in a family, that's a sort of holy communion, and you'll know it when the time comes, because you'll feel God there."

He looked over at Mama, rocking quietly with the baby at her breast. At that moment, as if feeling his eyes, Mama raised her own, and I intercepted a look so private that I felt at the same time both awed and intrusive, and very glad to be their child.

"Don't you worry," Pa said to Celinda. "I'll see your Pa tomorrow. I'll make sure you're all right. Meanwhile you let Tish take you up and put you to bed."

Marnie helped me propel Celinda upstairs but she soon vanished, sensing she wasn't wanted. Celinda had retreated into some inner fastness that shut even me out. She moved stiffly, like an automaton, and it wasn't till I got her undressed that I realized why. Mrs. Dodds must have taken a leather strap to her. There were long welts and purple bruises across her breasts and back. It took a long time to get liniment on them, for though I tried to be gentle, Celinda flinched at every touch. She hadn't heard a word that Papa had said, I thought. Afterwards, in bed with the light out, she lay stiffly by the edge instead of snuggling up for security the way she usually did. I lay on my side, feeling sick inside, and fell asleep thinking up suitable tortures for Mrs. Dodds.

Celinda was still asleep the next morning, the bruised circles under her eyes showing sharply against her wan face, when I went down to find the breakfast table atmosphere explosive. ". . . positively antediluvian!" Ben was saying. "Imagine anyone having such an unenlightened attitude in the twentieth century!"

"Imagine anyone having such a filthy mind!" I added darkly.

Marnie snorted. "She ought to have a daughter like Mary Lou Hodge if she wants something to really worry about."

"Come to think of it," Ben said speculatively, "a dose of Mrs. Dodds might do Mary Lou a world of good. Did you see the way she was rubbing her rump up against Doug. . . ."

"Little pitchers," Mama said warningly, shoving oatmeal at Missy, whose eyes were like saucers. We didn't bother worrying about Peter; he's far too engrossed in the sex life of insects to care anything about that of *homo sapiens*. But the conversation was shut off abruptly, for Celinda came in, looking like a mute and rigid little ghost.

We were still at the breakfast table when two things happened simultaneously. Kenneth arrived to walk me to Sunday School, and the telephone rang. I took the door, and Pa the phone. "Yes, she's here," I heard him say, and behind me at the table I felt Celinda stiffen.

"Sit down and start praying," I hissed to Kenneth, who didn't need prompting. He slid into the nearest chair and seemed to disappear into the woodwork. The rest of us strained our ears.

There was a burst of static from the other end of the phone, which Pa interrupted firmly. "No, I will not, Mr. Dodds. I suggest that you had better come over here. *Alone.*" He dropped the receiver back on its hook emphatically.

Celinda had turned grey and looked about to bolt, but she couldn't, not with Ben and me hemming her in on either side. Quite as if by accident, Ben's chair moved in closer, pinning hers in place. That instinct in Missy that makes her never miss a cue prompted her at that moment to wriggle up into Celinda's lap, leaky jelly doughnut and all. Even Cicero galumphed over to station himself behind her chair, head lolling hopefully, and his one visible eye firmly focused on the doughnut. Even at her bravest, Celinda's more than a little intimidated by Cicero's size, and she didn't look a bit brave at that moment. She clung to Missy for dear life, and her eyes were enormous pools of panic.

Mama refilled Celinda's cocoa cup. "Drink that. Nothing to be afraid of. Mr. Sterling's here. We all are."

"Mama . . . suppose Mama comes."

"She won't," Pa said. He was right, too; when the doorbell rang, Mr. Dodds stood on the porch alone.

That in itself was odd. Somehow, when we thought of Celinda's family, it was always *Mrs.* Dodds we meant. Without his mate Mr. Dodds still looked crowlike, but much less terrifying; more gawky and Lincolnesque and human. He came into the kitchen and got a look at Celinda, and his jaw dropped.

"Daughter, your *hair*! What have you done . . . the Bible says her hair is woman's crowning glory. . . ."

"Better tell your wife that," Pa drawled. "That there's her doing." He sounded as if he was enjoying himself.

Mr. Dodds, who had been about to speak, stopped and looked as if Cicero had just rammed him in the stomach.

"But . . . why?" he finally managed.

"So plumb sick in the head she thinks this poor child's a scarlet woman!" Mama, the undemonstrative, went over behind Celinda's chair and hugged her hard, like a mother bird prepared to defend her nest against attackers.

Mr. Dodds's jaw dropped again. Pa pushed a chair towards him. "Sit down, Mr. Dodds, and have a cup of coffee. I think you're going to need it." Mr. Dodds plopped into the chair as if hypnotized, never taking his eyes off Celinda. He'd had the stuffing knocked out of him, and high time, too.

All the time we were waiting for Mr. Dodds to arrive, I'd been busy marshalling a blistering attack, but I didn't need it. This was going to be my parents' fight. Pa and Mama made a thorough job of it, with Pa, deceptively calm and slow-spoken, providing the heavy artillery barrage, and Mama peppering his words with brisk bird shot.

Pa would have made a good lawyer. By the time he was finished, any jury in the country would have adjudged the Doddses unfit parents. Mr. Dodds had deflated down to human size, and Celinda was hiding her stricken face in Missy's hair. Pa dragged out a lot of past history that even I'd forgotten, and the very ordinariness of his tone made it all that much worse. Beside me Celinda shuddered once and was still, and I saw my mother's arms tighten around her.

"But . . . why?" Mr. Dodds looked at Celinda directly. "All this time . . . I know I haven't been home much, but surely you could have come to me, could have told . . . surely you knew I wouldn't want. . . ." Celinda didn't answer, and he turned back to Pa. "I came home on the train this morning . . . my wife was hysterical. Said the child had run away in the night. . . . I wasn't told a word about the rest of it." He looked at Celinda again. "In the middle of the night. We were sick with worry. Why couldn't you have waited till morning—till I was home? We could have talked. . . ."

"Because," Celinda said, "I was afraid if I stayed I might have killed her."

The room was very still. I looked at Celinda, sitting there so small and vulnerable, and I exploded. "*You* might kill *her!* How about the other way round!" Mama's hand grabbed my arm but I rushed on heedlessly. "How about the licking you got last night? It will take weeks for that to heal, and it's a wonder there's no broken bones." Too late, I realized the adults didn't know about that yet. My father and hers were demanding explanations simultaneously. Don't tell, Celinda's eyes begged mine, but I turned my face away resolutely. "She's been beaten. It looks like with a leather belt. Anyway, she's all over bruises."

The little muscle in Mr. Dodds's cheek began to flicker. "Is this true, daughter?" Celinda just closed her eyes. But her father was a man of action as well as of few words. He just went over and unbuttoned the back of her shirtwaist and looked for himself. Then he buttoned her up again, very gently. Nobody knew quite where to look, and I could hear the ticking of the grandfather's clock, unnaturally loud.

"Sick-in-the-head, sick-in-the-head," Missy hummed, making a song of it, from Celinda's lap.

Mr. Dodds turned to Pa. "Perhaps that's the . . . kindest explanation. I wonder if you'd be willing . . . obviously, I have some matters that will have to be worked out . . . if Celinda could stay with you for a few days."

" 'Course she can," Pa said promptly. "Best thing for her." He looked at his watch. "If you'll excuse us—I'm a Vestryman, I've got to get to church to usher. Celinda can come with us, if she'd like."

"No," Celinda said quietly, and we all jumped. Her hands were locked on the arms of her chair, until her knuckles showed white, but the words poured out of her in a torrent as though a dam had broken. "No. I've had church rammed down my throat since I was Missy's age. Don't do this, don't do that, or I'll go to Hell. Everything we do had got to be according to what God wants. Well, if God wants—*this*"— her fingers went to her bruised body—"then I don't want God, not ever again. I don't believe in Him any more. Because this is Hell, right here and now!"

"You want to answer her, Mr. Dodds?" Pa asked mildly.

Mr. Dodds shook his head, no more able to speak than I. I looked at Mama and saw that her eyes were very bright. Pa sat down in his chair, casual and relaxed, as if he'd forgotten he hadn't all the time in the world. "I'm an ordained elder, Celinda," he remarked, "so I guess once in a while it's all right for me to preach a sermon. And I reckon you're right, the ones we live are more important than the ones we preach. I'm not as religious as I might be, I suppose, and I reckon I don't know the Bible as well as your Pa and Ma, but I remember a verse I learned when I was about your age. 'What doth the Lord require of thee, but to do justly, and to love mercy, and to walk humbly with thy God.' Nothing in there about a lot of dos and don'ts, it's more an—attitude, a way of life. That's what I've tried to teach my kids. And there's something else, too, about the most—the only—really important thing being love: love of God, and love of your fellow man."

I felt Kenneth looking at me, and remembered the day last summer at Gramps's farm when I had first realized that he was someone special.

"Funny thing about love," Pa went on thoughtfully, as if to himself. "A lot of hurtful things get done in its name. A famous preacher once, named Jonathan Edwards, he went around preaching sermons on hellfire and damnation that are enough to curl your hair, but he did it out of love, because he didn't want people having to pay the consequences of their sins.

"Your Ma, now. I have to admit she has different ideas from Mrs. Sterling and me. But she wouldn't carry on so about you if she didn't care. Maybe God says different things to different ones of us, in different ways. And maybe we don't always understand so good. But we've got to try, according to our own inner light." He looked directly at Celinda. "And we've got to remember ourselves not to fall into the same pit we think others have done, if they've hurt us deeply. We've got to remember to hate the sin but love the sinner."

I figured maybe I could convince Mama to let me stay home from church this morning, along with Celinda, on the grounds that I'd already heard a pretty good sermon.

It worked, too, which is why I'm sitting in my bedroom now in a silent house, writing in my Journal and trying not to look at Celinda who lies on the bed, her face to the wall. I've learned so much from you, Pa, from you and Mama. But there are a couple of things you haven't taught me yet. Like, I can put liniment on her black and blue spots and they'll fade in time, but how can I heal the hurt she's got inside? How long will it be before she'll trust a boy, or God, again? And how do I learn to forgive—not those who've hurt me, but what is seventy times harder, the ones who hurt the people that I love?

CHAPTER FIVE

March

At 4:15 p.m. on the first Tuesday of March, my life changed dramatically. Not that I was aware of it at the time. At that precise moment I was more concerned with how I was going to convince Mama I had forgotten to come straight home from school that afternoon to baby-sit while she went to Ladies' Aid. I hadn't known when I made that promise at the breakfast table what was going to come up in between to make it highly inconvenient. But I knew well enough the peppery things Mama'd have to say if I called home and asked to be released, so I didn't bother wasting time to make the call. I knew, too, what I was going to hear when I did show up, which explains why by 4:15 I was worrying more about my own defense than about what impression I was making at the moment. That's probably why things worked out the way they did; I forgot to be self-conscious and to try too hard.

I'm getting ahead of myself as usual. February was over now. March had come in like a lion with one last sleet storm beating against the windowpanes. Celinda was back in her own house again. She had stayed with us a week. By that time her hair was beginning to grow in again. Mama gave it a good cut to even it off, and it curled in little tendrils around her face, lending her a fragile prettiness she had never had in her old taut braids. Her bruises were fading and the welts were starting to heal. But the new heart-stopping look in her eyes had not gone away. I didn't think it ever would.

Her father had come for her on Sunday afternoon and they had left together, seeming awkward and self-conscious with each other. I wondered how things were working out for Celinda in that eternally neat and silent house, but that was one of those things you couldn't ask. Celinda's mother wasn't home. Mr. Dodds had driven her away in the middle of the week, and it was given out in the neighborhood that she had gone for a "rest cure" somewhere in New England. There was no mention of her coming back. Neither Celinda nor her father spoke of her at all, and it was another of those things we couldn't ask.

"Best thing for all concerned if she *don't* come back," Mama said tersely. Mama had definitely taken Celinda under her wing, even though she never put her affection into words.

It seemed funny having the bedroom to myself again, and I was kind of glad whenever Missy burrowed in beside me during the course of her nocturnal wanderings, even if she did still have a disconcerting habit of wetting the bed. I didn't see too much of Celinda during the week after she went back home, for she was full of the responsibility of being her father's housekeeper.

"*Now* I understand why you were groaning so last summer," she whispered to me when we managed to sit together during morning exercises Tuesday. "Housekeeping's *work!*"

"Shhh!" Sourpuss Sadie was directing a fish-eyed stare in our direction, and I jabbed Celinda in the ribs. Mr. Moore was introducing Mr. Grimes who was, he said, going to make an important announcement. The student body, which had been degenerating into yawning restlessness, directed its attention. Anything new was bound to be of interest.

Mr. Grimes rose, fixed a look on Doug Latham who glowered and thrust his peashooter back into his pocket, and cleared his throat. "I'm making this announcement at the request of the president of the Browning Society. As you know, the Society has been going through some reorganization lately"—a knowing ripple spread through the assembly room—"and is hoping to—er, broaden its base and make a real contribution to the life of the school. Accordingly, the officers in executive session yesterday approved a plan to stage a dramatic presentation in the school this spring, and to open auditions to all students, whether members of the Browning Society or not. I have been drafted as the director." There were a few muffled catcalls and cheers, for Mr. Grimes is a popular teacher in the school. "In keeping with the—ahem!—the artistic and literary ideals for which the Society is noted, the play selected is *Romeo and Juliet*. Lots of blood, gore, murder, and suicide. Old fogey parents. I trust the language won't offend the fainthearted."

The audience, which had become restive at the mention of Shakespeare, began to look interested again. "A lot of fighting, which means we need good athletes. We'll be working out the fight scenes in the gym. Anyone squeamish need not apply." Mr. Grimes was a regular Machiavelli. Already I could see the school's recognized athletes eying each other furtively, checking the idea out. "There is only one catch. The play will have to be presented early in May, so all you scholars will have ample time to concentrate afterwards on the matter of final exams. That means we have to get started very soon. In fact, today. We hope all of you, especially underclassmen and those interested in English and history, will come out." Mr. Grimes's gaze roved purposefully over the assemblage and rested for a moment, speculatively, on Stella and me. It was at that moment that I decided Mama's Ladies' Aid meeting could just go hang.

You need not guess about the prime topic of conversation the rest of that school day. Speculation on casting was immediately rampant. A certain faction was convinced that the cast was already picked, and that open auditions were only a ruse to keep people happy. "Even Grimes isn't dopey enough to try something like Shakespeare unless he knows he has people good enough," was how Charlene put it. "You need real talent to make Shakespeare interesting."

Everybody was pretty much convinced that upperclassmen would get the leads, for they had both experience, prestige, and presence. Besides, it seemed only fair.

Mary Lou tossed her curls. "I don't know. After all, Juliet wasn't yet fourteen." Mary Lou must have been doing some fast reading that morning to uncover that fact; I was sure she'd never dipped into the play before. "Of course, no one *really* as young as fourteen could do it justice," she added hastily. "It needs someone just a little older, who understands life."

"You mean who knows what it feels like to lose a boy? I suppose you're trying out," Stella said silkily. Some of Stella's comments go clear over people's heads, but everyone knew that Mary Lou and Doug had been having problems lately. Mary Lou flushed.

"Mr. Grimes knows he can count on the regular Browning Society crowd; he knows what they can do and knows they won't walk out. But he's so kind he can't help feeling sorry for the people outside."

With this lovely start, by a quarter to three everybody was

in a charming state of nervous tension. Mrs. Owens had to snap repeatedly to get attention. A flourishing correspondence in illegal notes was making its way up and down the aisles.

Celinda had flatly refused to go with me to tryouts. "If I go, you'll be at me to read aloud, you know it. Or Mr. Grimes would. I'd die first."

"*I'll* die if I have to walk in alone. It'll be all upperclassmen and dear Mary Lou."

"Isn't Kenneth going?"

"He says he likes to read plays, not get up and act them out." The real reason, I suspected, was that he still suffered from shyness and the burden of being "Doug Latham's little brother," but I was not about to utter this aloud. "*Please*, Cee!"

"Oh, get Stella to go with you!" Celinda exclaimed waspishly. "She's got confidence enough for ten."

Stella also, I remembered, had a lovely reading voice. Oh, what was I getting so worked up about, anyway? As a freshman I hadn't a prayer of getting a part.

The three o'clock bell rang, and I found Stella, and we made our way together to Mr. Grimes's classroom. Mr. Grimes was conferring with the Browning Society president, and two other officers were busy bringing stacks of small navy-bound volumes from the bookroom. Within a few minutes the room began to fill—upperclass girls; a sprinkling of immature boys; Anne, looking scared; Mary Lou, accompanied by Charlene and looking self-important. Finally a group of the school athletes entered in a body, trying to cover their self-consciousness with guffaws and laughter.

Mr. Grimes distributed the little navy books. "I will hear you each read both a dialogue and a soliloquy. There are many roles, so if I ask you to read one it does not mean I will not also be considering you for all the others. Now who is brave enough to volunteer first?"

Mary Lou's hand shot up. She was assigned a selection and began to read in her best school elocution manner, with many flourishes and dramatic pauses. There were a few muffled groans, and the athletes looked as if they wished they hadn't come. Mr. Grimes interrupted in the middle of a sentence. "No, Mary Lou! This is all new to Juliet, she can't sound as if she thought it out and practiced it before. She's young, and excited, and more than a little scared. She's just been to her first grown-up party, she's just gotten her first crush on a boy. Now she's found out he's her family's mortal enemy. How would *you* feel?" He held her with a penetrating look from which she could not escape. Mary Lou colored slightly and dropped her eyes, and when she began again she sounded different, with most of the bravado gone.

Stella looked speculative. "You know, she's not half bad."

I hated to admit it, but it was true.

Auditions dragged along; a lot of upperclass girls tried out, and tension built. There were embarrassed titters as people stumbled over Shakespearean lines and made hash of iambic pentameter. Anne read, inaudibly—she was scared to death. Stella read; she was good, too, as I had expected, although her brisk matter-of-factness seemed out of the character. But she, like everyone else, improved under Mr. Grimes's suggestions. The clock ticked inexorably on. Mama, I realized uneasily, was going to be absolutely furious.

"Want me to wait to walk home with you?" Stella whispered.

"Please! I'm going to need support!"

Mr. Grimes had turned his attention to the athletes and they were reading the Tybalt scene. They were pretty awful. Anne leaned over. "I don't know how Mr. Grimes can hope to do this thing if he can't find some better boys!"

"What this scene needs is kids like Ben and Doug!"

"Fat chance!"

We began to imagine the earlier scene, in which Romeo and Mercutio mock the nurse, with a cast composed of my brother, Doug, and Mary Lou. Stella's eyes were dancing. "Do you know what those lines *mean?* My brother studied this in college, and he told me. Listen!" She whispered a brief and bawdy explanation. We all blushed. The aisle rocked with our mirth. "It's very appropriate for Mary Lou," Stella gasped, wiping her eyes.

I came to with a start to hear my name being called. "Tish! I asked you to read the Juliet-Nurse scene in Act III. That is, if you're still interested. Stella will read the nurse."

We scrambled furiously to find the place. It was easy reading with Stella because we knew each other, and Stella's genuine warmth shone through the lines. But I was doing poorly and I knew it. I had started too fast, I was gabbling like an idiot. A shadow flitted across Mr. Grimes's face. I stumbled on a line and heard, distinctly, Mary Lou's patronizing laugh. I stopped abruptly.

Stella's hand closed hard around my wrist and she whispered sternly, "Don't let her get to you! You can do it, Tish. Take a deep breath, and start over when you're good and ready."

I closed my eyes, and when I opened them again, Stella's own clear brown eyes held them. Stella gave me the cue again, and she didn't sound like she was acting, she sounded like Stella being real. The nurse was telling Juliet, "He's dead!" and I remembered what it was like when I thought Marnie was dying. I thought what it would be like if it should be Kenneth, if I was never going to see him again. And a queer thing happened. I forgot about Mr. Grimes, and Mary Lou, and the seniors listening. I forgot that I was reading for a play.

I was just talking, to Stella who cared too, about something that mattered very, very much to me. When we finally finished, I found that tears were running down my face. I felt like an utter fool.

"Thank you, Tish," Mr. Grimes said in a queer voice, and called on somebody else, and I turned to Stella.

"Let's get out of here. I'm going to get killed." Stella and Anne had heard all about the difficulties I was about to have with Mama. We walked home while I rehearsed my defense. I was doing a lot better acting job just now than I had done at tryouts. Anne and Stella tried loyally to reassure me, but I knew quite well I hadn't lived up to my own standards for Tish Sterling. At least Kenneth hadn't been there to see, but I was sorry I had disappointed Mr. Grimes. I tried not to think about the seniors and Mary Lou Hodge.

When I got home, it was nearly five o'clock and I didn't have to try at anything, because Mama was so busy telling me how she wasn't speaking to me that nobody could get a word in edgewise for two hours.

"Might have known I couldn't count on you . . . one-track mind . . . don't care beans about your family . . . trying to make an impression on everybody else . . . don't know why I bother. . . ." It was Mama's lecture #6341, which all of us kids could have repeated in our sleep. To get back in her good graces and to salve my conscience, I took over with the little kids for supper and bedtime, and Missy lured me into telling stories, and after that I remembered a little matter of a Latin assignment. Since I was in no shape to face a Sadie Albright tongue-lashing on the morrow, that meant a late-night session.

By the time I was finished, it was almost midnight. I decided a little pre-slumber nourishment might be in order and tiptoed down the stairs. Mama, who was still undergoing the trial of two a.m. feedings, was long since asleep, but a ray of light arrowed from under Pa's study door. The door opened as I was starting back upstairs balancing a collation of milk, bread-butter-and-sugar, and two Kosher pickles.

"Feel like fixing me some sustenance, too?" Pa suggested hopefully. "Then you might come in and tell me what your Ma was so het up about this evening."

I fixed a duplicate of my little snack, and we settled down sociably in front of the dying coals. Pa listened with interest to my comedy of errors. "Don't you think you might have made a phone call?" he asked. "Just in the interest of family peace?"

"Pa! You know what Mama'd have said. Then if I'd disobeyed and stayed anyway, I'd *really* have been in trouble. I'd rather have heard the lecture than missed the tryouts."

"I see your point," Pa conceded.

"I might as well have come home anyway." Depression settled again like a sudden fog. "One of the upperclassmen is bound to get the part." I hadn't realized I'd been thinking only of Juliet, but this was so. "If not, it'll be Stella who has the brains, or Mary Lou who's got the looks. I really disgraced myself."

"It's only a school play, after all," Pa said mildly. "Nobody ever claimed that we were actors, so you haven't let the Sterling name down none."

"It's Mr. Grimes I'm really sorry for. Pa, those boys were awful! The play needs to be good to show everybody the Browning Society's not just a lot of social-climbing snobs."

"And Mary Lou needs that part to live down the plagiarism disgrace," Pa said shrewdly. "Mark my words, if she doesn't get it, she's going to kick up quite a fuss."

I hadn't thought about that before. Celinda and I discussed

it on the way to school Wednesday morning, and the subject of the play itself was hashed over thoroughly by the whole crowd during lunch. The general consensus was that in attempting Shakespeare, the Browning Society was biting off more than it could chew. I began to stop thinking of myself and started feeling quite sorry for Mr. Grimes.

The rest of that week was like an installment story in the penny papers—a new crisis every day.

On Wednesday afternoon, word spread that several of the upperclassmen had been asked to return for private readings.

On Thursday Ken met me after first class, grinning wryly. "Mr. Grimes asked me to reconsider trying out. For the honor of the school and Willie Shakespeare and all that."

"What are you going to do?"

"I don't know," Ken said ruefully. "Darn it, he really made me think."

Thursday was further enlivened by a knock-down-drag-out row at lunch between Doug and Mary Lou, who was clinging to him like a leech. Mary Lou wanted to talk to him in private, and all Doug wanted was to escape to masculine freedom with his cronies. It ended with Mary Lou storming in tears to the Girls' Cloakroom and cutting her afternoon classes. Doug was so unnerved that he actually let Mr. Grimes twist his arm into coming in after school to discuss the play. He was accompanied, naturally, by my brother and several of our local hoodlums.

On Friday, Mary Lou was playing the Tragic Queen, and the girls were so busy listening to her tribulations we didn't have time to think about the play. Kenneth decided he was being selfish if he held back when Mr. Grimes needed him. The rumor spread through the school at dismissal time that the play might be cancelled because of lack of a suitable cast.

On Saturday, rain poured down from every corner of the sky, raw and chill. Our roof leaked, which didn't improve Mama's disposition. Doug came over in search of Ben, and they spent most of the day in the attic, playing cards and telling each other ribald stories. Marnie tried to crash the party and was kicked out, which is how I found out about the ribald stories.

Mary Lou came to church on Sunday looking as if she'd been crying. Doug did not walk her home, and he did not escort her to Young People's that night. By the end of the evening the girls were holding a council of war in the church kitchen, because Mary Lou was acting like an absolute bitch. She was chasing after everything in trousers, even Kenneth, which was perfectly absurd. And I was getting jealous, which was sillier yet. Ken and I almost had a fight ourselves on the way home, but fortunately I recovered my sanity in time.

By Monday the crowd was divided pretty evenly into two camps, those who thought Doug was giving Mary Lou a raw deal, and those who thought she was getting exactly what she deserved. Since it was a toss-up who had been using whom in that particular combination, you could pretty much pay your money and take your choice. Doug was getting so hot under the collar about everybody minding his business for him that he forgot himself to the extent of telling Mrs. Owens to go to hell, and was promptly suspended from school for the balance of the week. This information bubbled rapidly through the school, concurrent with the news that Mr. Grimes was posting a cast list for *Romeo and Juliet* on the bulletin board at three p.m.

"So Mr. Grimes was able to put a cast together after all!"

"And oh, my dears," Celinda said profoundly, "if Mary Lou doesn't get a part, today we are really going to feel the earth shake. She needs it bad."

Kenneth took no part in these interesting discussions. He was worried about what was going to happen when his parents found out about Doug's latest suspension. Being related to Ben and Marnie, I could appreciate exactly how he felt. He cut out quickly as soon as the dismissal bell rang. "Sorry, Tish, I've got to get home and tell Ma and find out where Doug is. It's a safe bet he didn't go straight home."

Anne and Stella and I met in the cloakroom and, accompanied by Celinda, made our way downstairs to the bulletin board in the main front hall. Quite a crowd had congregated when we arrived, not only those who had tried out but others as well. Most of them were seniors whom I did not know. My skin felt clammy.

"Well, you would try out," Celinda said unsympathetically, but she squeezed my hand.

"And we all know the parts will go to seniors, anyway. Oh, well, here goes." I gritted my teeth and followed Stella as she competently pushed her way through the crowd. Once within reading distance, I was afraid to look. If Mary Lou Hodge got that part, I thought, I'll die. If it's Stella, I can be happy for her. But I knew I'd rather lose out to a senior than to either of them; I'd feel less like a failure.

"Tish," Stella's voice said quietly, "you got it."

Celinda, who had pushed in beside us, was bubbling with repressed excitement. "Tish, wake up. *Look!*"

I did look, and there was my name, unmistakably printed. *Juliet . . . Letitia Sterling.* "I don't believe it," I whispered. Stella hugged me hard. And then it did sink in on me, and I let out a whoop, and the upperclassmen who'd been acting disgruntled that a lowly freshman had walked off with the plum suddenly got excited for me, and the noise got so great that Mr. Moore, smiling, poked his head out of his office to see what was going on. Finally I pulled free and ran down the hall and out into the street where I didn't even feel the March wind blowing. I ran towards home, with Anne and Stella and Celinda at my heels, and all I could think was, *Thank you, God!* over and over.

"Did either of you get anything?" I finally thought to ask.

Anne shook her head. "We didn't really expect to. Everybody thought it would be mostly seniors. But I'm so glad you're in!"

"I told you you could do it," Stella said. "And isn't this one up beautifully over Mary Lou Hodge! I cannot like that girl to save my soul."

"Who's playing Romeo?"

"Didn't you notice?" Celinda's eyes were dancing. "It's Ken."

My cup of joy was running over.

How long does it take for a balloon to burst? I ran into the house, flinging down my schoolbooks every which way and hollering, "Mama! Everybody! I got the part!" And Mama, darning socks in the parlor, didn't even bother looking up as she said matter-of-factly, "Guess not very many folks tried out."

I stared at her, and the only thing that prevented my shouting Marnie's favorite hell-and-damn was the lump in my throat. I ran up to my room and slammed the door, and banged things around a little, and then Marnie came in, demanding to know what was wrong. So I told her.

"Oh, you know Mama," Marnie said practically. "Don't let her ruin it for you. She didn't mean to. Come on, let's go down and tell Bron."

Bronwyn's enthusiasm soothed my wounded spirits, and so did her devil's food cake and tea, but they couldn't restore the fragile confidence that Mama's words had wiped out in a single instant. The irony was that Mama obviously didn't have the faintest notion of what she'd done.

"Can't understand it. Should think she'd be on top of the world," I heard her say bewilderedly to Pa.

"You know Tish," Pa said calmly, puffing his pipe. "Always been sensitive. That's why she's bound to be a good Juliet." Pa's confidence was a rock for me to cling to.

The telephone rang all evening with calls of curiosity and congratulation. Celinda called to see if I'd come down to earth. Stella called to say Mary Lou was absolutely green, and even if it was awful of us to feel that way, wasn't that just dandy? Ken called, sounding rueful. "Guess I should have stayed to look at the bulletin board after all. Oh, well, at least you're playing opposite me so it won't be all that bad." Which was a left-handed compliment if I ever heard one.

It wasn't till the next day on the way to school that I pieced together who was in the rest of the cast. Ken and I were the only freshmen, which was natural, since we were playing the youngest characters involved. Most of the other roles were played by seniors. The president of the Browning Society was Friar Lawrence. Mary Lou was nothing, and I was malicious enough to like that fine. I would not have enjoyed the ordeal of rehearsing with Mary Lou.

"It serves her right, anyway, the way she's been acting," Celinda said callously. "Maybe not getting her own way for a change will improve her character!" It was rare for Celinda to be so ruthless, but the worm was beginning to turn. Mary Lou had been making remarks lately about Celinda's mother being sent off to the looney-bin, and Celinda'd heard them.

"And Doug," said Kenneth, "is playing Tybalt, which should be interesting."

It should indeed, in view of the conflicting emotions Romeo had to feel over Tybalt's death. There were potentials in this play to shake us all, I thought, and shivered.

"What's the matter?" Ken asked.

"A mouse ran over my grave."

"Doug won't be able to come to this week's rehearsals, because he's on suspension. Mr. Moore told him one more complaint against him, and he's out for good. Only they can't very well throw him out now without sabotaging the play for Mr. Grimes."

"Maybe Doug will behave," I said hopefully.

Ken snorted.

That afternoon, after bidding farewell to various well-wishing friends who seemed disposed to stay and watch but were sent firmly on their way, Ken and I attended first rehearsal. I went in feeling shaky and eager; I emerged discouraged, scared, and thoroughly confused. After the second rehearsal I was in the clouds, drunk on words, on excitement, on playing opposite Ken who was beginning to find confidence and to enjoy himself. We coasted through the rest of the week being delirious together.

The honeymoon, as the saying goes, was brief.

My first intimation of storm clouds came at Young People's on Sunday night. Mary Lou was being very much the Tragic Queen, subdued in suffering, her witchy mood forgotten. I found this out from Celinda on the way to school on Monday; I hadn't paid too much attention at the time. As a matter of fact, I hadn't been thinking of anything but the play.

"We noticed," Stella said drily.

"We?"

Celinda flashed Stella an odd look. "Oh, everybody knows

you're in a fog right now," she answered lightly.

I was in such a fog that I'd forgotten Mr. Grimes's weekend assignment. He detained me after class to remind me that extracurricular activities were no excuse for missing work, and I was enormously embarrassed.

Rehearsals, without warning, became just awful. For one thing, it was difficult just moving so many inexperienced people around the stage. For another, Doug was there. In his presence Ken dried up, became stiff and awkward. I ached with him but couldn't say a word. And to our humiliation we both found we couldn't play the love scenes opposite each other. We just couldn't, that's all.

It wasn't that we didn't try. I'd have kicked myself black and blue if it would have helped. I'd tell myself—and I knew Ken was doing the same thing—that it was perfectly silly, that everyone knew it was just a play. Then we'd get up there, with Doug's knowing eyes upon us, and I'd see Ken growing wooden, retreating into his shell the way he'd been before this year. And as for me—afterwards, just thinking about it, I'd grow hot. Every time the play called for him to touch me, for a second I'd be back in that blasted pantry closet with Herbie Willis's breath upon me, and I'd flinch. It would only be for a split second, but it would happen. I couldn't help it, and I hated myself for what I saw it do to Ken.

Celinda called, too casually, to ask how everything was going. I was immediately suspicious. "Why?" I demanded. "What's been going around?"

"Oh, nothing," Celinda said hastily. "It's just we never get to talk at all, you're so busy with rehearsals." A pause. "I suppose," Celinda said delicately, "that rehearsals are getting rough. I guess that's natural around this stage."

I didn't answer. At the other end of the wire I heard Celinda give a little defeated sigh. "Well, if you want to talk any time, you know where to find me."

I wished I could talk, but I couldn't, not about this. Anyway, with Celinda so terrified of men to start with, if I told her what I was feeling I'd shock her out of ten years' growth.

Marnie had burst into the kitchen and was pantomiming violently for me to get off the phone. The moment I hung up the receiver, she exploded. "Do you know what that skunk Mary Lou is doing now? She's telling everybody the only reason she didn't get your part was because you made up an awful lie about her signing her name to something she didn't write. And that the reason you did it was because you knew about the play way last fall and wanted to make sure she didn't get the part!"

I stared at her.

"Nobody," Mama said calmly, ironing, "is fool enough to believe anything Mary Lou says. And folks around here know Tish too well for that. Besides, look at Viney Hodge and what happened at the school. All blew over."

"People believe things they want to hear," Marnie said darkly. "No, Mama, I won't hush up. Tish needs to know so she won't get hurt. A lot of the kids think Tish is the Girl Who's Got Everything this year. They're jealous of her brains, and her marks, and the special things that've happened while she's a freshman, and her being teacher's pet with Mr. Grimes and Mrs. Owens."

"Where'd you hear this?" I asked through stiff lips.

"Down at the soda shop. Jimmy told me I ought to go and listen. He thought it was mean. Oh, Tish, I'm sorry, but somebody had to tell you."

"Thanks at lot," I said quietly, and turned, and went upstairs and locked the door. I lay on my back on the bed, staring at the ceiling. Marnie was right, it was necessary for me to know. But I hated her all the same for telling me.

CHAPTER SIX

March

A lot of the kids resented me, Marnie had said. I wondered which ones they were. The ugly little worm of suspicion made me doubt everyone, so that I was snappish on the way to school next day, even to poor Celinda. Surely not Celinda, who'd been my best friend all my life. Not Stella—but Stella's shrewd eyes could see deeper into people's motives than they could see themselves. Not Anne—but Anne had wanted a part in the play herself, and hadn't gotten it. Not Ken. . . .

In history class I received a public call-down because I hadn't done a major report. "Tish, I thought you understood that you had a responsibility to keep up your work. Extracurricular activities are no excuse." I could feel every eye in the room upon me.

By lunchtime I'd have gone off on a crying jag if anybody'd given me a cross-eyed look. By afternoon rehearsal I had the shakes. We were up to the tenderest scene between the lovers, and Doug wasn't there, but just the same I froze, even before Ken touched me. Mr. Grimes sent everyone else home and tried with us alone, but it was still no good. Finally Mr. Grimes tossed his script aside and sat down on the edge of his desk. "All right, you two, suppose we talk about what's bothering you. Something is, I know."

Ken looked rather white around the lips. "Maybe you ought to get another Romeo. I wouldn't mind. I told you I'm not an actor. And I don't want to ruin the play for Tish."

"Ken! It's not you—"

"It must be. You're great in every scene, except with me. That is, till today."

"That's just it. *I'm* the one who shouldn't be in it." To my shame, I felt tears sting my eyes. I turned away and fought them back.

Behind me, Mr. Grimes said quietly, "Want to talk about it?"

"I can't." I was putting up walls, but I couldn't seem to help it. And Kenneth was hurt, I knew. There was a silence.

"Go home and sleep on it." Mr. Grimes sounded tired. "Tomorrow at rehearsal we'll have to work out something. Otherwise—" He left the phrase unfinished.

I wasn't up to walking home with Kenneth, not with this hanging unspoken in the air between us. I ran out to the sanctuary of the Girls' Cloakroom where he couldn't follow. Behind me I could hear voices in the halls—it was still early, and over the winter kids had formed the habit of loitering in the halls. I pulled on my old winter coat, worrying so hard about how I was going to set things right with Ken that I didn't stop to brood, as usual, over how much its dark brown color extinguished me. The coat was a hand-me-down of Bron's, and I wished she could have handed me down some of her confidence along with it. That was it; I would go over and talk to Bron. I'd die of shame explaining the whole thing, but Bron would understand.

I scooped up my load of books and emerged into the corridor

just in time to hear a dulcet voice say, "Hey, you in the orphan asylum coat!"

Mary Lou Hodge. My heart sank. Her dulcet tones were all I needed to put the crown and topping on this day. If I'd had any sense, I'd have kept on walking. But some perverse imp within me stayed my legs, made me respond distinctly, "Are you addressing me?"

Mary Lou smirked, and I realized despairingly that I'd betrayed the fact that she'd drawn blood. One for you, you rotten witch, I thought; one of these days I'll give you such a smack. . . .

". . . Know what you are?" Mary Lou was saying. "You are the most conceited girl in the whole ninth grade. I'm not the only person who thinks so, either. You know who else? . . ."

"Ssst!" somebody hissed. "Here comes Sourpuss Sadie!"

I should have cut and run just then. Instead, fool that I was, I let Mary Lou's beckoning finger lead me, and a whole flock of fascinated bystanders, into the Girls' Cloakroom again. Mary Lou slammed the door and leaned against it.

"I've been wanting to tell you this for a long time," she announced with satisfaction. "Now you're going to get it. The way you've been sashaying around the school acting like you're something great 'cause you're in the play . . . showing off your vocabulary . . . buttering up to Mr. Grimes. . . ."

"I don't know what you're talking about," I retorted with dignity—I hoped. To my shame I heard my voice quaver. I was *damned* if I was going to cry in front of Mary Lou Hodge! I clenched my fists until my nails dug circles into both my palms. One good thing about concentrating on self-control was that it distracted my attention from the meaning of Mary Lou's barrage of words. Then one phrase penetrated loud and clear.

". . . throwing yourself at all the boys . . . think they think you're so great . . . Herbie Willis told me. . . ."

My eyes flew open and stared straight into hers. I felt my whole body shaking. Dear God, I wondered, what had Herbie said?

I wrenched my eyes away and found myself focussing on the brocade lining of Mary Lou's flossy new coat. I closed my eyes and still could see the pattern. For the rest of my life, I thought, I'm going to be able to draw the blue violets from the black lining of Mary Lou's coat. And all the while the barrage of Mary Lou's words battered on and on. I have never in all my life felt so terribly alone.

Then, blessedly, something happened to break the spell. The door behind Mary Lou was pushed open and Mrs. Owens's voice, tolerant and amused, said, "Honestly, don't you children ever go home? You clear out now!"

As if by magic, my legs could move again. They carried me past Mary Lou, who was still foaming at the mouth, and out the door and down the hall, almost without my own volition. Without volition, too, my own mouth was working. I heard my own voice, like a stranger's, saying fiercely, "Drat and blast! *Damn* that Mary Lou Hodge . . . a cheap two-penny slut . . ." and a whole lot of other words I'd found in Pa's old books, which I'm not supposed to understand, except I do.

Vaguely I was aware of other people in the hall, of hands reaching out to me, but I kept on going. I kept on all the way out the building and down the hill and finally into Vyse Avenue and home.

Marnie was standing in the kitchen, making herself a graham cracker and jelly sandwich, when I entered. She took one look at me and her jaw dropped. "Well!" she said in astonishment. "What happened?"

"That Mary Lou Hodge!" I flung my books violently across the room and my Latin book broke its binding against the kitchen stove. Sourpuss Sadie wasn't going to be happy about that, I thought dully. I felt my body starting to shake again. And all of a sudden the control to which I'd clung so precariously all the way home dissolved. I burst into tears and collapsed with a wail into one of the kitchen chairs.

"Oh, lordy, Tish, what's wrong?" Marnie sounded alarmed. "You want me to get Ma? She's over at Bronwyn's. I can run and get her."

"Don't you dare!" I yelled hastily. The tears choked me again, and I buried my head in my arms. Cicero, as usual when anyone's upset, forgot he wasn't a lapdog and tried to climb aboard to give comfort, and we ended in a tangle on the floor, me and Cicero and a scared, concerned Missy, who burrowed between the two of us and wailed in sympathy. I buried my face gratefully in Cicero's mop of wool and just let go.

By the time the rest of the family arrived home, I was over the worst of the weeps and had managed to escape upstairs. Presently I heard Ben's voice mixed with Marnie's, sounding outraged, and Mama's, being brisk and decided. I heard Mary Lou's name being mentioned, but Marnie must have succeeded in communicating my mood, for the family, with heavy-handed tact, forbore any mention of her over the dinner table. Everybody was being rather deliberately witty, and ignored the fact that after the first couple of mouthfuls I stopped eating because I couldn't swallow past the lump in my throat.

Twice during dinner I was called away to the telephone. Pa, who thinks such interruptions are a tarnation nuisance, frowned the first time, but I heard only a muffled "Ow!" and knew Ben must have kicked him under the table.

The first caller was Celinda, speaking in a breathless whisper. "Pa gave me permission to call 'cause I said I had to check a homework assignment. Tish, are you all right? I spoke to you in the hall but you walked right past. You looked like death warmed over."

"I *feel* like death warmed over. I got trapped into a Moment of Truth with Mary Lou Hodge."

"I know," Celinda said. "I was outside the door and heard. Tish, I'm so sorry. I wanted to stop her but I didn't have the guts."

For Celinda to use a word like that was a measure of her concern.

"That's all right." I hoped I sounded calm and brave; my stomach wasn't feeling like it one bit. "Actually, I didn't really hear very much. My ears sort of rejected the sound."

"Well, everybody else heard," Celinda said. "Loud and clear. Golly, I never knew that cloakroom could hold so many people. Neither did Mrs. Owens. She chased everybody out, and then she got Mary Lou into the classroom and got the whole story out of her."

"You're kidding!"

"No, really! Mary Lou was hanging around with me as if she wanted to talk. I think she was embarrassed."

My mind boggled at the thought of Mary Lou being embarrassed by anything, but Celinda never lied.

"Of course," Celinda added ironically, "Mary Lou told the whole story as if someone else had done the telling off, but Mrs. Owens wasn't fooled. She told Mary Lou she had a right to her own opinion, but not a right to air it unkindly, or to air it at all unless she was doing it as an act of love. Mrs. Owens threw in a lot of stuff about history and civilization to disguise the dose, but Mary Lou got the message all right."

Mary Lou must have. The second call, some fifteen minutes

later, rocked me off my feet. The voice coming over the wire was rather stiff and queer, but it was indisputably Mary Lou herself. "Tish, I want you to know I'm sorry. If I hurt your feelings, I mean. I still think you're conceited, but I shouldn't have said the things I did." She hung up before I could reply.

Well! I thought, putting down the telephone receiver. I wondered what I was supposed to make of that.

I slept better than I had expected to, thanks to those two calls. By the time I reached school the next morning the queasy feeling in my stomach had half-subsided, although my apprehension deepened as I went indoors. I was aware of a crowd parting, of covert whispers, as I entered the Girls' Cloakroom. Mary Lou was hanging up her coat at the far end of the room, but we ignored each other with the expertise of Ma and Aunt Kate. I caught a glimpse of myself in the little mirror, and wished I hadn't. Mary Lou was right, that dratted coat *did* make me look like an orphan.

I felt a lot better when Celinda and I emerged from the cloakroom, for Kenneth was standing there, obviously waiting. Without a word he took my books, tucked my hand through his arm, and marched me off to our first class. Such physical contact is definitely frowned upon by the school authorities, but Kenneth, the usually shy, acted as if he didn't even notice. I was delighted to see that Mary Lou and her bosom companion, Charlene Snead, had been hanging around the hall and witnessed the whole thing. I was also entranced, on noting our reflections in the glass of a door, to see that Ken was now a good head taller than I. We didn't, I thought with satisfaction, look half-bad together. Then I remembered Mary Lou's crack about throwing myself at boys, and the reference to Herbie Willis, and I felt sick and cheap.

It was obvious that the tale of our fracas yesterday had not only spread but grown in telling. Most of the students brought their lunches to avoid the icy walk home, and when we gathered in the Social Room at noon, the place had the atmosphere of two armed camps. I felt as if I were back in ancient Rome when the Christians were being thrown to lions, only I wasn't sure whether Mary Lou or I was supposed to be the victim.

Ben did something unheard-of. He not only voluntarily came over to eat with me, his sister and a girl to boot, but he brought his whole crowd as well. Doug Latham may have the worst reputation in the school but he is undeniably cute, and moreover the whole school knows Mary Lou chased him all winter but now seemed to have lost him. The boys' joining us reshuffled the seating quite a bit at our table. Ben ended up next to Stella, and didn't seem a bit upset about it. Mary Lou and Charlene ended up eating across the room with a few female hangers-on, looking absolutely green.

Sourpuss Sadie had the expected caustic remarks to make about my mutilated Latin book, and she added a few more when she discovered I hadn't done a lick of homework that night. Mrs. Owens was a bit more tolerant of the composition that I'd forgotten. At the end of the period I went up to thank her for talking to Mary Lou and to tell her of the phone call I'd received.

"One of these days that child will find out she's gone too far, and she'll get what's coming to her." Mrs. Owens grinned. "I gather you got a bit of your own back yesterday."

Good heavens, I wondered, what had I *said* to Mary Lou?

One fantastic thing that I didn't deserve had happened as a result of all this mess. Ken, in his protective anger, had either forgotten or was overlooking the strain in which we had parted the day before. In my other misery, I had forgotten about it myself. I remembered it when Mr. Grimes looked at us searchingly as we came into rehearsal together. It dawned on me that, with one thing and another, Ken had been touching me all day, and I had not only not flinched, I had clung to it and revelled in it. So why did I have to be so silly about rehearsals? Oh, damn Mary Lou Hodge anyway and her dirty mind.

Ken did look a bit wary as rehearsals started, and I could sense a dubiousness had crept into the rest of the class. And all at once my Sterling stubbornness came crashing back with a resounding roar. This show was not going to be a flop because of me. I wasn't going to give Mary Lou that kind of satisfaction. Or hurt Mr. Grimes that much, or Kenneth. Or, admit it, myself. Sterlings had too much pride to let things—inside or out—defeat them.

Mr. Grimes had evidently decided the best way to handle the situation was to act as if it didn't exist. He moved rehearsals along so fast we scarcely had a chance to catch our breath. Before we knew it we were in the middle of the lovers' farewell scene, and the same thing happened that had happened to me with Stella at auditions. It stopped being a play and started being real. Nobody else seemed to be there. I was I, but I was also Juliet, and Ken was Ken and Romeo, and I was afraid I was never going to see him again. And I wasn't holding back or building walls, I was giving with everything that was in me. Ken was holding me so tight I couldn't breathe, and I was yielding, and the tears were running down my cheeks.

When the scene was over, there was a moment of astonished silence and a spatter of applause. My eyes focussed with difficulty back on the twentieth century. Anne and Stella and a few upperclassmen had sneaked in to watch. Ken was regarding me with something like awe. I just felt limp.

"Don't stop. Keep going!" Mr. Grimes was forcing us on into the scene where Juliet learns she is to be married to the County Paris. Ken, whose part was over, was dismissed. The scene, with a build like that before it, gathered momentum and emotion quickly. When we were finished, Mr. Grimes said, "That was a very good rehearsal," in an odd tone, and let us go. I was still groggy.

Stella, I found, had waited for me and she coped with my vagueness, shepherding me firmly into the orphan asylum coat and out into the street. A soft rain greeted us, cutting through the mists.

"Well," Stella said at last, watching me, "what happened?"

"What do you mean?"

"Oh, come on," Stella said in good-natured earnest. "I'm not quite a fool. Ken's been a thundercloud all week, and you've looked like death warmed over. Besides, my brother's become one of Ken's best friends. And I was in the cloakroom yesterday. And everybody's heard that rehearsals have been rough. Today was anything but rough, and you're back together."

"I guess Mary Lou got me mad enough to stop being self-conscious." I glanced at Stella, remembering how her warm matter-of-factness had gotten me through auditions, and was moved to confiding. "It's queer—playing opposite Ken—especially in some scenes. I freeze up, and Ken thinks he's what makes me do it."

It was a garbled explanation, but Stella said, "Oh," as if she understood. Stealing a glance at her, I suspected that she did, indeed. We reached her house and she said, "See you tomorrow," and went in without further comment, and I went on home, bemused.

It was quite late that evening when the telephone rang, providing a welcome interruption to my Latin. "Tish, this is Stella. Listen, maybe you're going to kill me, but I talked to Ken."

"You *what?*"

"Don't sound so scared, I have some sense!" Stella laughed. "Ken was over here doing homework with my brother, and we got to talking. About the play, and yesterday afternoon, and all. I kind of communicated the idea that sometimes when a girl freezes up it's because she doesn't feel like freezing up, if you follow me. I don't know how you feel about his thinking that, but it seemed to make *him* feel much better. Tish, are you there?"

"Yes."

"Well, anyway, that's me, Little Miss Fix-It barging in. I hope you don't hate me."

"I don't," I said, and meant it.

After that things seemed to go a whole lot better. At least I didn't have to worry about hurting Ken. We had no more scenes together for the next two weeks, and that helped too. And an odd thing seemed to be happening. Wherever I was, a little circle seemed to form around me, kidding and joking, making sure I got my homework done, that I got to classes or rehearsals or home on time—even, I swear, that I wore my rubbers on wet days. When Celinda with gentle stubbornness told me for the third time that I couldn't afford to catch a cold, I went into the house not knowing whether to laugh or cry. "I'm surrounded by an army of mother hens!"

"'Pears to me you're surrounded by some mighty good friends," Pa said quizzically from behind his evening paper.

I was never allowed to be alone, to do anything foolish or get discouraged, to be attacked. Another odd thing happened too along that line. All through our neighborhood, all through the school, whenever the play was mentioned, or my name, someone always seemed to pop up with a good word in my direction. I learned about this from my loyal spies Jimmy Breidenbach and Marnie, from Ben, and even from Mama, who came home chuckling from Ladies' Aid. "Kate was like a cat on a hot stove, not knowing which way to jump. Torn between annoyance at hearing Tish get praised, and pride at hearing the Sterling name get the credit!"

Even Pa had to grin about that.

The guard of honor was composed of Celinda, Anne and Stella, and Kenneth, of course, augmented by Jimmy Breidenbach, Marnie, and Ben, and I had an idea even Bron and Mr. Albright had been called in. I suspected the brain behind the plot was Stella's. Pa was impressed with Stella. "Girl'd make a good trial lawyer," he said after she'd been to the house one night for dinner. "She knows how to stay calm and rational and logical on the outside when she's white-hot inside." Since this was an attribute that I decidedly lacked, I was beginning to admire Stella greatly for it.

The result of all these manipulations was that the tide of public opinion was beginning to be turned. From being the conceited kid who had everything and knew it, I was becoming the nice girl who had been misjudged through jealousy. The halo sat uneasily around my ears.

"Oh, you'll do something soon enough to blow it," Celinda said soothingly. "Land knows you're no saint."

"Thanks a heap," I retorted with spirit. "But honestly, Cee, ever since that slanging match it seems like something's been making folks believe everything I said about Mary Lou—whatever that was!—and nothing *she* said! It's queer."

Celinda and Anne exchanged glances.

"Well, it stands to reason you'd be believed," Stella said. "Everyone around here knows the Sterlings are nice kids and the Hodges aren't."

She said it matter-of-factly, without editorializing, but I shot her an uneasy look. What Stella said was true, that was exactly what people thought. Only there was something wrong about the whole set-up somewhere. You couldn't just pin flat labels on folks like that. There was another reason they'd believe me, too—because they wanted to believe the worst of Mary Lou. So long as people could sit back and write the Hodges off as a "bad lot," and click their tongues, they could comfortably avoid the uneasy feeling I was having right now, that all of us were sisters under the skin.

I didn't like thinking about the whole situation, and I tried to blot it out with Celinda's staunch assurances that it would blow over, somehow, and with getting lost in the world of sixteenth-century Verona.

Romeo and Juliet was progressing surely. The Browning Society held a cake sale to raise money for yard goods for the costumes. True to the intention of "broadening the base," Mr. Grimes and Mrs. Owens had roped in kids from all through school to help with these. Anne was making two of mine; they were being copied from famous paintings of the period. At home Mama was in her semi-annual sewing dither. She was making me a new Easter suit with sleeves slashed fashionably at the elbow to let the undersleeves of lace peep out; they reminded me of the pictures I had seen of my Juliet costumes. But the hat Bron helped me to pick out was strictly modern, a large Leghorn straw drooping in front and back and garlanded with pink roses. It made me look, I hope, alluringly romantic and a good bit older. It was the most expensive hat I'd ever owned, a splurge from Pa in honor of my getting all A's on my last report card.

I just prayed I was going to be able to maintain those lofty scholastics during the current marking period, what with the play and all. If I did, the credit was going to be due to Celinda's nagging and to a couple of teachers for consideration above and beyond the call of duty.

Mrs. Owens asked me to come in to discuss the subject of my English assignments after school one Friday. I couldn't get there till after play rehearsal, which was pretty late. I went in apprehensively, wondering what on earth she wanted and hoping she wasn't going to raise too much Cain because I hadn't done the last composition assignment quite the way that she'd described.

"Sit down, Tish, and don't look so scared!" Mrs. Owens looked up, smiling, from the pile of compositions she was correcting. "As a matter of fact, this paper is quite good, even though I suspect it does deviate from being completely about a real experience, as I requested."

"I—sort of combined things here and there and heightened the dramatic effect."

"It *is* quite dramatic." Mrs. Owens's eyes twinkled. I'd written about hearing that Mama'd been at death's door in a trolley crash, which was a considerable exaggeration of what really happened. "It's good, vivid writing, except for structural errors that I expect you to correct. But I really wanted to speak to you about future work. You've been working under quite a load this spring. Would it help you to have a list of my assignments, for say, from now until the play is over, so you could work on them whenever you have the time?"

And God bless you, Mrs. Owens, I thought, smiling radiantly. With them, and a little luck persuading Mama I had sick headaches on non-rehearsal days, I could stay cozily at home from school and get the major part of my responsibilities done ahead. It might not be too honest, but it certainly would help the situation. I thanked her effusively and left the warm brightness of her classroom for the dim echoing stillness of the hall. The school was deserted on Fridays at this late hour. As I went into the cloakroom for my coat, thinking how glad I was that I'd only be wearing it a few more weeks, I heard the tapping of Mrs. Owens's French heels and the whisper of her skirts receding down the corridor. She must have stayed late only to talk to me.

I turned towards the cloakroom door and there, effectively cutting off my exit, was Mary Lou Hodge.

"I've been waiting for you. I want to talk to you."

"What about?"

I realized with a sinking sensation that I shouldn't have given her an opening, for she closed in firmly. "About the things you said about me that day—the stories you've been spreading around the school." With no audience around, Mary Lou wasn't bothering about what impression she was making. Her cheeks were an unhealthy red and her eyes looked driven. She must have been hanging around waiting to waylay me ever since school got out. "There's only one person you could have gotten that stuff from, and that's Doug. He won't tell me what he's been saying, so you've got to."

"My mother's waiting for me." I tried to duck past her out the door, wishing fervently that Mrs. Owens hadn't left. Mary Lou grabbed my arm so hard that her fingernails bit my wrist.

"Oh, no, you don't. I've been trying to talk to you for over a week, but your sweet little pals wouldn't let me near you. You're not getting away from me this time. Not till you tell me exactly how you knew. Did Doug tell your brother? Is that it?"

"I don't know what you're talking about!"

"Oh, yes, you do. Those things you shouted at me in the

hall. That's what this all started from, or are you too dumb to know. And I've got to find out exactly what you heard."

I was beginning to feel thoroughly frightened. "I didn't hear anything, I don't even know what I said—things I'd read in books. I was so mad. I was just yelling. Nobody'd believe me."

"Oh, yes, they would. They do. They think," she mimicked savagely, " 'The Sterlings are such nice people. That sweet little Sterling girl couldn't say a thing like that if it wasn't true.' You and your saintly goody-good pillar-of-church-and-community family! You make me sick!"

I remembered some things I hadn't thought about for years —Mr. Hodge carrying home a pail of beer from the saloon on Saturday nights, Mrs. Hodge trailing blowzily around in a wrapper at mid-day, the fact that Mary Lou and Viney always seemed to hang around other kids' houses instead of vice versa. I felt kind of sick myself.

"Mary Lou—honest—I don't remember what I said."

"You called me a whore," Mary Lou said bluntly. She released my wrist and pushed her hair back from her face. "Tish, can't you try to understand why I've got to know? I— love Doug," she said painfully. "I've trusted him. If he's saying—things like that about me, can't you see I've got to know? You couldn't have gotten it out of thin air, not you with your pure little mind. What *did* he say? Was it to Ben? Or Ken?"

"I don't know what you're talking about," I said. And then I stopped, staring at her, sick. Because all at once I *did* know. The pieces added up. One of the arrows I had flung blindly into the air had landed dead on target. *A whore,* I'd said. Well, maybe not a whore, in the technical financial definition of the term, but close enough. And everybody'd believed me, not because I'd known, not because it was true, but what was far worse—because it was what they wanted to believe. Mary Lou was right, we did have dirty minds. And for far too long I'd had my own head buried in the sand.

"You *have* to have heard something. You couldn't have made it up. And it couldn't have come from anyone but Doug." Mary Lou broke off, staring at me oddly. "You really didn't know, did you?" she whispered. "Not till I just told you. Here I've been imagining—worrying—and you didn't even. . . . Ha ha! It's funny, really. Oh, God, I'm going to be sick." She stumbled into the girls' lavatory, and I followed.

The last thing in the world I ever expected to be doing, on that or any other day, was kneeling on the dingy tiles of a lavatory cubicle holding Mary Lou's heaving shoulders while she was very sick indeed. I held her till it was over and she was leaning, limp and trembling, against the wall; then I went and got her a glass of cold water and bathed her face. I sat down on the floor across from her and neither of us knew where to look.

"Tish," Mary Lou's voice was low. "I'm not used to begging, least of all from you. Please don't tell anybody. It's bad enough now."

I forced a glance at her. Both her masks were gone now, the tough one and the too-cute flirt. For the first time, I thought, I'm really seeing Mary Lou. She looked bedraggled and unlovely and very human. And afraid.

I had precipitated this mess—through ignorance, through hurt feelings, through not putting myself in someone else's place. Strangely enough, I could believe her when she said she loved Doug Latham. And, remembering a lot of things I didn't want to face, I could understand exactly what she was feeling. *Couldn't I?* And in that moment I knew exactly what I had to do.

I told her the story of Herbie Willis and the pantry closet.

All of it. "It may not sound like much," I finished. "All I can tell you is if the story got out, I'd feel exactly the way you do right now. I've trusted you with it, so you know you can trust me. Because if I tattle, you can too."

I went and got her gaudy coat and got her into it. That coat was like the Sterling chin-thrust, I thought: a bright banner of pride against unfriendly winds. We went outside into the misty rain and walked in silence towards Vyse Avenue and home.

Mary Lou thrust her hands deep into her pockets, and she didn't look at me. She didn't look at anything, but her head was high. I walked her to her house, and when we reached it she went inside without a word. I knew what she was feeling. I knew because it was happening inside me, too, as if she were an extension of myself.

I never knew I could ache so much with someone that I couldn't even like.

CHAPTER SEVEN

April

April dawdled by, all smiles and tears. I read that somewhere, and it's a very apt description. I am not referring merely to the weather.

I was narrowing down to living in a very small world—not selfish, but self-centered, although I certainly didn't think of it that way. Mama would have said I didn't really think. I felt, and that was all. My world was the play—its conflicts, its pressures, its emotions. Nothing else mattered, nothing else was real.

Putting on a play was harder work than I'd expected. I hadn't known you came home from rehearsal feeling as if your very bones were aching. That going through such strong emotions was as physically exhausting as shoveling snow. Or that you came home from rehearsals not to fall gratefully into bed but to shut up your inner self and go through the motions of regular family life. To sit up late, after two hours spent cramming Shakespearean stanzas, grinding out A-level essay assignments—not just through personal pride but because Sourpuss Sadie had started a rumor that Mr. Grimes was lowering the school's scholastic standards by diverting the children's attention into a tarnfool play. To have to do your best acting not onstage but off, because if you didn't act interested in the crowd's activities and gossip, your friends got mad.

Mama was pretty good-natured, all things considered, but she was irritated by my absentmindedness, and Marnie was frankly fed up with doing my forgotten chores. I couldn't blame her.

"I do them," she said bluntly, "because otherwise Ma would, and then there'd really be explosions. But enough's enough. I've got my own life."

"I'm sorry. I'm just so blasted tired."

"Too tired to take the trash out with you when you leave for school? You just plain forgot."

"I was up till three a.m. doing poetry analysis for Mrs. Owens. And don't you dare tell Mama!" I ran my fingers through my hair. "Why do we have to analyze poetry, anyway? Why can't we just enjoy it! And why do we have to read that kind of poetry in the first place? 'Two distincts, division none.' How can something be two and one at the same time!"

"Don't ask me. *I'm* not trying to be a genius," Marnie said pointedly. "You forgot something else too. You told Celinda you'd meet her at the Library after rehearsal. She phoned at six and said she couldn't wait any longer. She sounded hurt. Mama didn't call you 'cause you were doing homework. I was setting the table. It was your turn for that this week."

"Cee'll understand."

"Well, good for her. I'm glad somebody does." Marnie leaned forward earnestly. "Tish, if it's really too much, why don't you just quit?"

"Don't be silly!"

"Then stop killing yourself on schoolwork. The world

won't stop if you get a C for once."

I didn't even bother to answer that.

As a matter of fact, I was running for my life just to get a B sometimes. Somehow things said in class didn't register. I felt the way I used to when I was little and Mama gave me soothing syrup—half-alive. I'd have forgotten my head if Celinda and Anne and Stella weren't still keeping track of it for me, and I appreciated that enormously, but often I didn't even notice if they were around.

I did know of a few things happening in school—like the firecrackers set off in the chemistry lab, which nearly blew up the school. I was one of the four who knew it was Doug who'd set it, and that the only thing that had saved the school, and Doug, was Ben's quick action in putting it out and destroying the evidence before Mr. Moore even found out it all was going on. Ben was getting worried about the direction Doug was heading, so much so that he got him out behind the barn and gave him a tongue-lashing that was reinforced by fists. This was after the firecracker episode, and after the flaming row Mary Lou and Doug had outside the school one lunchtime that ended in him hitting her and shouting not to be such a blank-blank leech. I could have cried over that, and I felt like telling Mary Lou she was only making things worse, but I didn't dare. Especially since I wasn't supposed to know about any of this. I didn't learn it from the girls at lunch. I learned from Ken, in our private stolen whispers backstage, in our long slow walks home through the late spring sunlight.

Kenneth was a rock of reality for me to cling to in the chaotic current of my life. I suspected that I filled the same role for him. Mainly, I was a listening ear—apparently Ken had never had one before. I heard a lot more than he knew he said.

Kenneth too was worried about where Doug was heading. Unlike Ben, he didn't think it was all Doug's fault. "My folks let him get away with too much. They always have. Doug's never learned what it's like to have somebody stick to an ultimatum."

"Last week you said your father was too strict with him."

"Sure. Sometimes. But it's not consistent. So Doug always figures that it's worth the gamble, and if he loses he can always turn on his so-called charm." Ken looked at me. "When Ben and Doug got caught cutting school last week, what did your father do?"

"You mean after Mr. Moore got through with him? Grounded Ben for two weeks, and cut off his allowance permanently. From now on Ben has to earn his own expenses. Being suspended from the ball team was the worst punishment, though. Ben tried to tell Mr. Moore that that was unfair to the team, but Pa said Ben should have thought of that a little sooner."

"That's what I mean," Ken said. "*My* father yelled at Doug for three solid hours about how could Doug disgrace him like that, that he was killing Mother. Hanging wasn't good enough for him! Then next day Father went in and talked Mr. Moore into cancelling the suspension so that Doug could stay in the play. I'd have thought more of Mr. Moore if he hadn't given in."

"He *was* in a spot. It would have been awful for Mr. Grimes if Doug had to drop out."

"Which is exactly what Doug was counting on," Ken said promptly. "I wish just once somebody wouldn't let him get away with it. By the way, how come Ben cut with him? I thought he'd learned better."

I didn't answer. As it happened, I had demanded the same

thing, and Ben had told me that if it was any of my business, he'd gone along to try to keep Doug from getting into worse trouble than he was in already. I couldn't tell Ken that. I was only just beginning to realize how much he wanted to be able to look up to his older brother.

The space backstage, in the dusty musty auditorium with its piles of backdrop curtains, was becoming our private world. We flopped there for snatched moments of rest, worked on homework together when we weren't needed during scenes. Once I even fell asleep, but Ken woke me up before I missed my entrance cue. I suspected sometimes I was seeing *too* much of Ken. Our relationship was getting too all-engrossing. We were starting to know too much, to see too deeply. My world was narrowing down, and I was losing touch with the rest of life.

Mama was beginning to make noises along those same lines. "How many afternoons this week do you have rehearsals?" she demanded at breakfast. "None today? You come right home at three. Take Katie out in her carriage so I can go to Ladies' Aid. Take Missy, too. Fresh air and sunlight do you all good."

I'd planned to attend rehearsal anyway, since it was one of Ken's big scenes, but it didn't seem advisable to push the point. The girls looked at me in astonishment when I emerged from the building with them at three. "No rehearsal?"

I shook my head. "I have to take Katie and Missy for a walk while Mama's out."

"Let's all go," Stella said. "I'll run home and get Timmy. He's kind of old for strollers, but he loves the attention. We can take them to the pond and feed the ducks."

It was, as Mama pointed out, a lovely day to be outdoors. The sky and clouds looked as if they'd just been scrubbed and hung out to dry. Accompanied by one little brother and two small sisters, and provided with an assortment of provender for children, ducks, and selves, Celinda and Anne and Stella and I embarked for the pond. It lay around a bend from Cee's and my drainpipe refuge. On the corner nearest the street was a trampled lot where the boys played ball. The pond wrapped itself behind a grove of copper beeches, and between lay an acre that in another month would be a sea of goldenrod and Queen Anne's Lace. Now, weeds and ferns were just beginning to unfurl a tender green. An ancient turtle sunned himself on a rock. Dragonflies skimmed the pond's surface, and a mother duck was teaching her flock of puffballs how to swim.

I smiled at Celinda. "I'd forgotten how much fun this used to be."

"We ought to do it more often. Pack a picnic supper and bring the kids." Stella caught Timmy by his suspenders just as he was about to dive into the water. "Or have a picnic, just our crowd."

"Oh, well," Celinda said, "Tish is so busy. She won't have time till the play's over. If then."

There was an odd note in her voice. I sat up quickly. "I'm not *that* busy," I protested. "How about Saturday? Let's go downtown on the trolley and go shopping." This was a privilege we'd only recently been granted. Excitement fizzed through the air as we laid our plans. I got us home late for supper, and Missy was a muddy mess, but Mama didn't say a word.

It was a good thing that I had that break on Wednesday, because rehearsals the next two days were sheer torment. We'd reached the stage where nobody liked anything—the play, each other, Mr. Grimes, and least of all themselves. Thursday was bad enough. The rehearsal started late, and from that lovely beginning went downhill fast. Nobody was in the mood. They cracked bad jokes and found double meanings in all the lines. At five-thirty Mr. Grimes slapped his script down hard. "There will be an extra rehearsal of this scene tomorrow for all of you. *On time*. And you will stay as long as necessary to get it right." He strode out grimly.

Mama hit the roof about that, and so did the cast. Mr. Grimes wouldn't even listen. He rode Friday's rehearsal like a cowboy breaking a wild horse, and a lot of things got broken in the process. I walked out of there ready to quit the play, hating Mr. Grimes for what he was forcing me to see. This was after he'd ordered me sternly, "Go deeper! You're playing her like a little high school freshman."

"Juliet," I snapped back, fighting tears, "wasn't yet fourteen."

"Yes, but *Juliet* wasn't hiding in her innocence," Mr. Grimes retorted. "*She* wasn't afraid of coming out of Eden." It was at this point that I did crack, hating myself for breaking down, hating Ken because he saw it. When rehearsal was finally dismissed, I stormed offstage.

"Hey, calm down," Kenneth called, and came up behind me. "It wasn't that bad. In fact, it was pretty good towards the end."

"You mean I actually stopped being the high school freshman I am?"

"Don't get mad at me. *I* didn't say it," Kenneth said, and took my books. I wiped my eyes and took a deep breath.

"We all need what Mrs. Owens was talking about today. A chance to let our souls catch up with our bodies. Sometimes I wish to God I could just run away."

"Let's," Kenneth said. I stared at him. "Tomorrow's Saturday. Let's take off for the day. Outdoors somewhere. We'll make a pact not to talk about the play at all."

So the next morning, when the sun was just a rosy glow behind the apple tree, I crept silently downstairs and raided the larder for a picnic lunch. I left a note for Mama on the table, saying I'd be back before dark and not to worry. Actually, Mama was probably awake and feeding Katie, and she wouldn't mind, but the secrecy kindled the excitement. Already my spirits were rising.

On the corner I met Ken, also swinging a basket and carrying a slim leather-bound book. "Poetry. Mr. Grimes says we should read it, that it sets our relationship for the first half of the play." He grinned. "Oops. We weren't supposed to talk about that today."

Actually, we didn't. The day was somehow suspended outside of time. We walked, while the dawn was still rising, through the strange neighborhood where Hodel Resnikov had taken me in September. I showed him Hodel's house, gilded by the early sun. We walked clear to the river and climbed the rock cliffs till we stood looking down on the awesome grey waters of the Hudson far below. We laughed a great deal. We played follow the leader, and hide-and-seek, as if we were Missy's age. Finally, in the late afternoon, we found ourselves back in our own neighborhood in the park, near the pond. Ken knew a secret clearing, shielded by trees, where the pond water lapped gently against the russet rocks. We lay down on the spring grass in the quiet sunshine, smiling at each other, for a long, long time.

Ken read aloud the poem Mr. Grimes had given him. It was called "The Extasie" and it was definitely not something we'd have been allowed to read in school.

> *Our hands were firmly cemented*
> *With a fast balm, which thence did spring,*

Our eye-beams twisted, and did thread
Our eyes, upon one double string;
So to'entergraft our hands, as yet
Was all the means to make us one. . . .
And whil'st our souls negotiate there,
We like sepulchral statues lay;
All day, the same our postures were,
And we said nothing, all the day. . . .
Love . . . makes both one. . . .

It fit, perhaps in more ways than Mr. Grimes intended. We were silent for a long time. "Believe it or not," Kenneth said at last, "that was written by a very famous Episcopalian preacher, back in Puritan times."

I shivered slightly, though I wasn't cold.

"We should be getting home," Ken said. "Sun's going down." Neither of us made a move to go.

"I wish I didn't have to go back," I said finally. "Not yet."

Ken searched his pockets. "I've got a dollar. Let's go eat supper out." So, swinging our empty baskets, we rode downtown on the trolley. The stores were open late since it was Saturday night. With our last pennies we bought two big lollipops and walked up Vyse Avenue, licking them and holding hands. Mama decidedly would not have approved.

Mama met me in the hall when I slipped in, her face a study. But by some miracle she only scanned my face, said, "Go to bed. Need sleep," and let me be. She even let me sleep through church next morning. I didn't wake up till almost noon, still bemused, but lighter in spirit than I'd been in weeks. "Better stay home from Young People's too," Mama said incredibly. "Get your homework done and go to sleep early."

I woke on Monday morning feeling happy to be alive. "I think I'll see if Celinda can come for supper," I told Mama. "She can stay and watch rehearsal after school."

Mama nodded, pleased. "Miss not having her around lately. Making Stretchable Stew, she likes that. Maybe I can run up a marble cake, too." Celinda definitely occupied a soft spot in Mama's heart. "Better run," she added. "Late. Celinda'll have left."

"She won't. She always waits." I ran, humming to myself, out into the fresh warm April sun. To my surprise, when I reached our usual corner, Celinda wasn't there. It was odd for her to be late. I was debating whether I should wait when I suddenly spied her, with Stella, far down the street in the direction of the school.

"Cee! Stella! Wait!" I called, and started to run, but they neither slowed nor turned. They looked deep in talk, and as if they were doing fine without me.

Well! I thought, and slowed my steps. I hadn't been *that* late. After I slowed, I could have kicked myself, but it was too late. A little of the glow had gone off the lovely morning. Cee and Stella, with Anne in tow, were just leaving the cloakroom when I entered. That was the point when I should have said something, casually, but I just repeated Stella's abrupt " 'Lo," and the moment passed. For when I came out of the cloakroom, Kenneth was waiting for me. We just stood smiling at each other for a few minutes, and then we walked to the Assembly Room where Mr. Moore was already rapping for silence, and after that there was no further time for talk. The formal business of the school day had begun.

I did notice, as the day progressed, that Celinda seemed unusually quiet. But with one thing and another, I never had a chance to ask about it. And at lunch there was no opportunity for private talk. The air was fizzing with gaieties of the weekend past. I wasn't paying much attention to the chatter, but gradually it registered that somebody had had a party on Saturday night, that the excitement had spilled over into Sunday and still was high. A party to which I hadn't been invited.

Of course, I was out all day Saturday. Nobody could have reached me, I comforted myself. But Mama would have told me if anyone had called.

I swallowed and tried hard to look as if my roast beef sandwich hadn't suddenly acquired the taste of ashes. But I needn't have bothered, for everyone seemed to have forgotten I was there. They were teasing Mary Lou about her conquests at the party. "You really showed Doug! He's certainly got the message you're not pining over him, not after the way you were flirting at Celinda's house Saturday!"

Celinda's. *Celinda* had given the party and hadn't invited me. If it had been anyone else, my mind could have invented some pride-saving excuse. But not Celinda.

As far as I was concerned, the rest of the day was a horror. I snapped at Mama when she asked why Celinda hadn't come home to dinner. And if I cried myself to sleep that night, there was no one there to see.

By morning my hurt had hardened into a cold lump of pride. That day it was I who started for school early and alone, and who did not stop nor turn when Celinda called. I felt like a rat for a moment, but the feeling soon vanished in the harsh light of the realistic thinking I could not avoid.

Celinda'd had a party . . . that in itself was something. She'd never been able to before, even if she hadn't been too shy. In the back of my mind I must have known that someday, now that her mother was gone and she was growing up, she'd start to socialize like the rest of us. But if so, I'd comfortably assumed that I'd be the mastermind behind the scenes, that Celinda would need to lean on me as always. Only apparently she not only hadn't needed me, she hadn't even wanted me there. And that cut deep—clear to the bottom of the rock of confidence on which I'd built my life.

Perhaps it was fortunate that school that day was laden with unpleasant tests. I didn't have much time to think. Rehearsal afterwards was pressured, too. We were unsure of everything—our lines, each other, ourselves. Even Kenneth's patience was fraying as he struggled with one of his long speeches. After rehearsal Mr. Grimes carried Ken off to work on the speech in private, and I got the distinct impression they didn't want me to wait around. I looked for Mrs. Owens, but she had already left, so I wandered out, feeling forlorn, into the April afternoon.

It was funny, really. I would have laughed if I hadn't been so close to tears. For weeks, pressured beyond believing, I'd longed for an afternoon free. Today I had one, part of one anyway, and didn't know what to do with it. I didn't want to go home, that was sure. People there were apt to ask embarrassing questions. Mama was still trying to find out why Celinda hadn't come to dinner. So I set off aimlessly up and down the streets, trying to beat out my tangled thoughts.

I felt acutely and completely rotten. I felt lonely and unnecessary and thoroughly unloved. And the worst of it was I didn't know the cause. Celinda had never acted like this before. I must have done something, only I didn't know what, so anxiety and anger battled in my heart.

Pride said let them go, you don't need them. Only my insides didn't agree. Pride said act like nothing's happened, never let it show, and my eyelids stung with trying to obey. I walked and walked, while all the thoughts I'd managed to avoid in school hammered insistently for admission to my mind. I may be sensitive and imaginative and given to escaping to daydreams, but I'm a Sterling too. And that means having a hard core of reality that won't let me avoid facing the truth, no matter how hard I try.

The truth was that I was being deliberately snubbed—not by Mary Lou Hodge, not by outsiders who could comfortably be overlooked on grounds of jealousy or lack of understanding—but by my closest and dearest friends. The very persons whose faith and loyalty and love had rallied round so unswervingly just a few short weeks before. They couldn't all be misjudging me, much as my battered pride wanted to believe it.

I found myself crossing the street at the corner of my own Grace Church. Melodrama suggested I go inside and lick my wounds in solitude awhile. Reality told me that idea was fake and sentimental. And Ben's occasional comments about the hypocrisy of Christian love were uncomfortably close to my own feelings at the moment. I started determinedly down the street past the church, in the direction away from home. And then I stopped as my legs began to turn to jelly.

There in the dappled sunlight of the churchyard were Celinda and Stella, sitting on one of the white stone benches. Piles of books, and their spring coats, were scattered on the grass. They were deep in conversation and were obviously getting along fine without me. I willed some stiffness back into my legs and crossed to the other side of the street, so I wouldn't have to acknowledge them as I passed. Not that I expected they were going to let themselves see me, either, but there is such a thing as pride.

They were just about safely behind my line of vision when I heard a sound that, as the penny paper novelists would say, chilled me through. It was Stella's voice, level and challenging, saying, "Don't say hello!"

I turned, reaching for Aunt Kate's dignity. "I hardly thought it mattered."

"Phooey," Stella said bluntly. She sounded exactly like Marnie. "Come over here, Tish."

"What for?"

"So we can talk." She saw the expression on my face and added, deliberately, "Unless you don't dare."

That did it. I marched across the street and plunked myself in front of them, arms folded over my schoolbooks like an advancing shield. "All right, I'm here. What do you want to talk about?"

"Don't *you* know?" Stella demanded.

"No."

"I don't either." Celinda's voice was high. She wasn't looking at either of us. Gradually, through my wariness, percolated the realization that a tension existed between her and Stella. Celinda's walls were up a mile high, and Stella was being a bit too brisk and bright. She was trying her staring-into-one's-inner-soul routine on both of us; Celinda avoided it and I just stared right back. Minutes ticked uncomfortably by. Finally Stella jumped up, spilling her pile of books. "You two make me sick! You're both going around like Roman martyrs, and you won't even try to talk it out. What's the matter with you, anyway?"

"It's none of your business," I retorted icily.

Normally saying anything like that to Stella would get an instant comeback, but today Stella wasn't playing. "I'm making it my business. I may not have known you long, but I know you both well enough to know this isn't like you. You've been best friends for years!"

"Some friend!" I blurted out. "She even had a party Saturday night and didn't ask me." I hadn't meant to say that, and stopped abruptly.

"I didn't think," Celinda said in a voice like a little silver knife, "that you would care to come." I just gaped at her, and she went on, in that unfamiliar voice, "You obviously didn't want to spend the day with Stella and me Saturday, or you wouldn't have stood us up."

I stared at her blankly.

"We were going downtown shopping," Stella said drily. "It was your idea. Don't you remember?"

The bottom dropped out of my stomach. "Oh, Cee! I forgot all about it! Ken and I both needed to get away, so we just—went off. But I didn't mean to stand you up. I honestly forgot."

"That's the whole point." Celinda was starting to tremble, but her eyes were determined. "You forgot, that's how important it was to you. That's how important *we* are to you, any more."

"Cee, that's not true!"

"And here we've been knocking ourselves out trying to help you. I guess that shows how much we matter to you." Celinda's voice went on like a mechanical toy that had been wound too tightly and could not be stopped. "I needed to go downtown to buy a present for my father's birthday Sunday. I waited till Saturday so we could go together. Only I never got there 'cause we stayed home all day, calling your house every hour to see if you'd gotten home. We wasted the whole day waiting. That's when we dreamed up the party, to have something to do. I didn't bother telling you, since you'd gone off without bothering to remember us."

"You do that, too," Stella said quietly. To my surprise, she was looking at Celinda. "Lots of times. To and from school. If I'm not there first, you two just go off together and forget I exist. You do it to Anne, too, and it really hurts her, though she'd never say it. Sometimes I've called after you, and you haven't answered. I tell you it makes me feel pretty small."

"Like I felt when you did it to me yesterday," I said. "It wasn't the first time, either."

We stared at each other in silence. The wind went out of me, and I gave up and dropped down on the bench opposite Celinda. "What's happening to us?" I said at last, slowly. "Each of you—I thought was a good friend of mine to start with. I wanted you to be friends with each other, because Celinda's never made friends easily, she's always needed me. Only now it seems like you two are friends, and you've shoved me out. And Celinda doesn't need me any more."

Celinda stood up, and she was shaking. "It's my fault. Like the old saying, two's good company and three's a crowd. You two are so much alike. You're both outgoing—and determined —and popular. I'm not. I never have been. I used to blame it on my parents, but it's not their fault, it's me. It's just the way I am. Tish has been trying for years to make me into something I'm not, but I just can't do it. It'd be better for everybody concerned if I just bowed out of the picture and left you two to be friends together." She stumbled away a few steps, her back to us. Stella and I looked at each other.

"I'm the one that's in the way," Stella said in a low voice. "You two were getting along fine till I moved in. Somehow I've got in the middle and messed the whole thing up."

"You can't take all the credit!" I started to laugh, a little hysterically. "I'm the one who forgot about Saturday. I'm the one who's been taking you all for granted. And not just you two, either." My mind roved back over the crowded month.

"Come to think of it, the universe *has* been revolving around me an awful lot, lately. I guess I never should have tried out for that blasted play!"

Stella shook her head impatiently. "Oh, stop dramatizing. It isn't—"

She had no way of knowing that using that word was like waving a red shirt before Gramps's prize bull. Before she could go on, my voice burst from me like a stranger's. "Oh, stop always analyzing me! You always think you can bust in and set everybody straight. Who are you trying to be anyway? God?"

I was totally unprepared for the violence of Stella's reaction. She gasped, staring at me, her eyes enormous. For a moment she actually seemed not to breathe. Then a choked sob broke from her and she bolted into the church. The door slammed shut behind her.

Celinda had swerved around, startled, at my outburst. We gazed at each other across the green peace of the churchyard, and I felt exactly the way Pandora must have when she opened up that blasted box.

"Dear heaven," I whispered, "whatever did I say?"

"Just the plain truth. Maybe that's the trouble. It obviously has some special meaning for her." Celinda came back and sat down on the bench. "Now what?" she said.

I didn't know. Two instincts warred within me. Common sense and my own chickenheartedness told me to get out of there and let bad enough alone, that too much had been said already. The Little Miss Fix-It side of me told me that was too easy an excuse, that I had no right to wield an ax if I wasn't willing to stay around and pick up the pieces. Before my nerve could fail I marched over, opened the door determinedly, and went inside.

It took a moment for my eyes to grow accustomed to the

stained-glass dimness. Then I saw Stella, her back to me, half-way down the aisle. Though she hugged herself tightly and was bent double with effort, she still couldn't hold back the shuddering soundless sobs. She looked so much like Marnie at that moment that I acted by sheer instinct. Despite my scaredness, I went up behind her and put my arms around her and hugged her hard.

"Don't!" Stella broke away violently and moved a few steps off. Her control broke and she started to cry. I heard her mutter, "Oh, damn," between hiccoughs and sobs, and I thought, now she's going to hate me for this, too.

My own voice sounded cracked when I tried to speak. "Stella, I'm so sorry. Awfully. Won't you please let me help?" I waited. "Or at least tell me what I've done? It's more than what I said. I may do stupid things, but I know that much."

"You couldn't help it." Stella gulped hard and got her voice under control despite the sobs that wracked her.

"I could have helped it. If I hadn't been so busy defending myself. I guess it was really myself I was attacking. And that's the God's truth."

Stella's lip curled mirthlessly. "Which one? God in heaven or God Molloy?"

"Stel, don't."

"I'm sorry." Stella banged her fist against a pew. "That's what did it," she said at last. "When you said that. It's something I've always hated—in other people. Then to think—that people could see *me* doing the same thing—" She made an angry, inconclusive gesture. "That's what hurt. Like you said. I'd thought, I really thought you liked me. Then to find out you could think that little of me—"

"Did it ever occur to you that we might still love you even if we do think you try to act like Mrs. God?"

"*I* couldn't," Stella said uncompromisingly.

"Oh, Stel! Maybe we all hate most the things we're afraid of admitting in ourselves." I took a deep breath and rushed on before she could explode. "Like what you said about me dramatizing. You were right. But I hate like hell admitting it. Especially to myself."

"Touché." Stella dropped down in the pew in front of me and flung her hair back from her tear-streaked face. "I don't know why I hate it so when people are like that—conceited, know-it-all. It—gets my back up. But at the same time, I've got this—compulsion, to get in and fix things up when I see they're wrong." She looked at me ironically. "Like you do—coming in here just now. I couldn't respect myself if I didn't. But I can't respect myself, either, when people see any weaknesses in me."

"Stella," I said, slowly, "does that mean you don't have any respect at all for me? Or for Celinda?"

"Of course not!"

"You've just got finished seeing weaknesses in *us*."

"But that's different. If anything, it makes me care about people more. I want to get right in there and help them." Stella stopped. "Oh. I see what you mean. I do have double standards."

"Join the club." Celinda had been right in recognizing the sistership in Stella and me. We had the same compulsion to achieve, to always be the best; the same contempt for inadequacy in ourselves and compassion towards it in others; we both needed love and reassurance and despised ourselves for needing what we loved to give.

"You were right," I said, "about the Roman martyr bit. I know I've been a real pill lately. I can't seem to help it. I'm so blamed scared. About the responsibility of the play—and what you were saying—not being able to live up to my own standards. Needing reassurance, and hating it."

"Oh, well," Stella said ambiguously, "it'll all come out in the wash, I guess. We'd better go home." She stood up, and I followed her out of the church. Celinda fell in beside us, and we walked to our respective houses, talking—when we talked at all—of trivia. Nothing had been settled, not really.

Come out in the wash? Perhaps. But some things were indelible. Too many things were being said that should never have been put into words, and having been said, could never be forgotten.

CHAPTER EIGHT

April

I got the devil from Mama for not coming straight home after rehearsal that afternoon, and I got it all over again, for being sullen, when I declined to offer any explanation.

"We're damned if we do and damned if we don't," I stormed to Marnie as we did the dishes. "If we explain, we're arguing; if we don't, we're sulking. You can't win around here!"

"Oh, it's not all that bad," Marnie said comfortably. "Stop dramatizing."

"Don't you *dare* say that to me!"

Marnie jumped. "Don't take *my* head off. What's got into you, Tish?" Her eyes narrowed. "Oh. Did you by any chance have a row with the girls this afternoon?"

"Whatever gave you that idea?"

"I'm not deaf, dumb, and blind-like some people," Marnie retorted. "You know you've been heading towards it ever since Saturday."

"Don't tell me you knew about that, too!"

"Who didn't!"

"Me, that's who," I said bitterly. "Thanks a heap for letting me in on it."

"And have you light into me like you did just now?" Marnie asked bluntly. "No, thanks. I figured you'd find out when you were good and ready." She wrung out the dishrag, hung it up to dry, and looked me over. "You look beat. You start your homework and I'll finish here. Want me to come cue you on your play lines later?"

Knowing how Marnie loathed that chore, I appreciated the magnificence of the gesture. "Thanks anyway. I'd better study them alone first. I'm lost on the long speeches." And on a few other things, too, I thought, dragging myself in search of my scattered books.

In the hall I encountered Pa, standing in his study doorway smoking his pipe. "What's the matter?" he inquired. "You have about as much steam as Cicero when he's just been spanked."

"That's about what I feel like," I answered grimly. To my chagrin I felt the tears, which I'd successfully kept at bay all day, begin to form again behind my eyes. "Oh, Pa, I've been such a fool."

"What'd you do, kill somebody or tell a lie or promise something you can't produce?"

"None of them. Told too much truth and had a one-track mind."

Pa nodded. "That could do it, all right. Care to come in and fill me in on some of the depressing details?" He stood aside to let me precede him into the study. It was the one room in the house where none of us were allowed without express invitation—not even Mama, whose compulsive tidying of Pa's business papers drove him wild. I plopped down on the Indian-blanketed sofa and Pa discreetly shut the door.

"Those two things you mentioned can be blessings or curses, depending on how they're used, in my experience. I take it you told a few unpleasant truths and got back a few about your involvement in the play?" I nodded miserably. Pa handed me a clean handkerchief and smiled whimsically. "If you were Ben, I'd offer you a smoke to cheer you up, but I don't think you'd cotton to it much. Tish, I don't want to start the faucets working, but do I dare suggest you have been getting a mite off-balance where the play's concerned?"

"Oh, Pa, I know it. I can't seem to help myself." I wiped my eyes, while he looked away tactfully. "Pa, remember the things we talked about, the night of tryouts? About how the play had to be good, for the Browning Society and for Mr. Grimes? And about what Mary Lou would do if she didn't get in? It was true, all of it. I knew playing Juliet was going to be hard, but I didn't know how hard."

"Are you saying it's not worth the effort?"

"Pa, of course not!" I stopped. "I guess I'm scared. Scared stiff. I didn't realize it till I heard myself saying the words this afternoon. Being Juliet's such a big responsibility, and trying to be *me*, too, at the same time—I expected Mary Lou and Company wouldn't understand, but not the others. . . ." Loyalty forbore my naming names. I took a deep breath and came down at last to the final truth. "I'm afraid I'm not going to be good enough, that I'll let everybody down. Most of all myself. I don't want to make a fool of myself and disgrace the family."

"Tish, stop that," Pa said sternly. "Are you trying your durndest? Not just with Juliet, but with all the rest? Then that's all that matters. You have to rely on that, and on the fact that your Ma and I have faith in you, even if you don't. That's what a family's for, to have faith in us when we can't have it in ourselves. And don't pay no mind if your Ma's been snappish. You know well enough by now that's just her cover-up."

He came over and put his hands on my shoulders and drew me to my feet. "I have faith in you, Tish. Remember that. No matter what happens. Now you go get your beauty sleep. I've got papers to correct."

I went upstairs feeling considerably lighter at heart. Pa had a knack that way. It wasn't till I was lying in the dark with my hair wound on rags and my face slathered with bleaching cream—I was trying to overcome deficiencies in both respects in time for the play—that I realized I had never even said thanks. I guessed I was more Mama's daughter than I wanted to admit. It was funny, I could get up on the stage and reel off flowery lines without the least self-consciousness, but when it came to saying something nice to someone close I'd rather be drawn and quartered. I got up and lit the lamp and dug out pen and paper and wrote a poem about it. When it was finished I read it over and decided it wasn't bad, in fact it was one of my best and it was a shame I couldn't show it to Mrs. Owens. I copied it neatly and slipped downstairs and slid it under Pa's study door, then went back to bed to the best night's sleep I'd had in days.

My good mood lasted through breakfast the next morning, enhanced by the fact that the curlers had done their work quite well. I started getting uneasy as the time to leave for school approached. Nothing had been settled in that little fracas at the church, and well I knew it. I made darned sure I was the first one at the corner, and that I waited there till Stella and Celinda and Anne had all arrived. I had no idea what to expect from Stella, but she looked and acted just exactly as if nothing had even happened. With reluctant admiration I was forced to admit to myself that Stella was either a better actress than I was, or a bigger person.

As soon as we reached school, the multiple pressures of the day descended on us, and I found my fragile security fast slipping away. Sourpuss Sadie was being her poisonous worst; Mr. Grimes was irritable; Mr. Moore chose that morning to call an unscheduled assembly for a heart-to-heart threat on the subject of spring fever. My mood was not improved by the note Stella passed me down the row: "Did you know Ben and Doug cut chemistry this morning?" She knew about it because her brother Larry was in their class, of course.

I passed the message on to Ken, and his face darkened. "So Grimes is going to have to go out on a limb for Doug again. Why can't the stupid bum stay out of trouble till the play is over! Oh, well, it's only a week or so!" And then, "Holy Je-hosophat, Tish, don't start to cry! I was only trying to cheer you up!"

It was hard to believe the play was only one week off. Re-hearsals now were running late. Next week, when we would be going through the entire play each time, they would be held at night, a prospect that did not enchant Mama. She'd been muttering, "Stuff and nonsense, child's too young for that kind of responsibility," which did not exactly heighten my confidence. Neither did the discovery that afternoon that I was still getting mixed up on the potion soliloquy, despite the hours I'd put into it the night before. The result was that the scene, which I was scared to death of anyway, kept getting more and more melodramatic. By the time we got to the end of the rehearsal my tears, although not Juliet's emotions, were absolutely real.

"Cheer up," Ken said consolingly, "the audience'll love it anyway."

"Pigs don't care if they are fed corn!" I said brutally. "But I care. And so does Mr. Grimes. And you do, too."

Ken avoided my eyes. "Mr. Grimes must have done a lot of talking to Mr. Moore today. My beloved brother is still in the play."

"He's good, too," I said honestly. "He's a perfect Tybalt."

"Oh, sure," Ken said ironically. "All Doug has to do is be his own complicated self. It's perfect casting." He gazed moodily across the room to where Doug was turning on his celebrated charm for the benefit of the senior girl who played Lady Capulet.

"Tish, *when* are you going to come try on those costumes that I'm making?" Anne had edged in between us, her soft voice apologetic and harried. "You were going to do it two days ago, but you forgot."

"Oh, Anne, I'm sorry. . . ."

"I know you're busy," Anne said without rancor. "But I'm the one's going to get the devil if they're not done by Saturday. Why don't you come home with me now and stay for supper? I can help you run those lines later, if you want."

I started automatically to say I was too busy, then stopped, remembering something Stella had said. I owed it to Anne after having been so rude—and besides, I really wanted to. "All right," I said impulsively, "I'd love to. Come on!"

The heavy red and white ball gown, and the filmy lilac for the elopement and tomb scene, were spread out carefully across Anne's canopy bed. I was stunned at their splendor, and even more stunned when Anne had laced me into the ball gown and turned me towards the mirror. The spreading, high-waisted white satin skirt was stiffly encrusted with hand embroidery of pearls and silver. It made me move, without any effort, exactly the way I should. And by some miracle Anne had contrived, with the close low-cut red velvet bodice, to give me the exact high-bosomed pouter-pigeon effect of old Italian portraits. I could hardly believe my eyes.

"Your hair goes back and up, like this," Anne said, behind me, "with these pearls across the forehead. . . . Do you think it's all right?"

I found my voice. "It's—absolutely gorgeous. I had no idea you could sew like this. It must have taken you forever!"

Anne flushed with pleasure. "After all, you have to look good. You're the one everyone's going to be looking at!"

There it was again—the responsibility. Oh, how I was beginning to loathe that word!

The first full run-through of the play was Saturday, and it was also our first chance to work with all the scenery, costumes, and props. Or at least it was supposed to be. Every two minutes something else turned up missing. The kids' spirits, which had started high, began to grow taut. Anne's costumes, I was delighted to note, made an instantaneous sensation. I was also not too harried to notice Ken's reaction to my own appearance.

"Very Botticelli," he said approvingly, checking over the lilac sheer. "I'm supposed to have a satin number to match with that, but it isn't done yet." He ran a finger around the ruffled edge of his lace-trimmed shirt. "I feel like a fool in these frills and tights!"

"You look terrific!"

Ken grinned. "So does friend Tybalt, and does he ever know it!"

All the boys looked good, and very different from their usual selves. They were covering up their self-consciousness with horseplay, and the comedy scenes took on decidedly ribald overtones. Aunt Kate and Miss Albright were definitely going to be shocked. Pa, I didn't worry about, but I wasn't too sure about Mama. Maybe, I thought hopefully, it will just go right over her head.

I probably need not state that the first run-through did not live up to our grand appearance. Mr. Grimes had to yell a few times, and there was grumbling from Doug Latham and his cohorts. There was more grumbling when Mr. Grimes announced that there would be a complete run-through every night the next week. "And we're going through the complete play, if it *takes* all night! So remember that and don't waste any time!"

I decided it would be a good idea to break that little item to Mama gently.

It was, all in all, a week beyond describing. Suffice to say that the entire gamut of tempers and emotions was run on the average of ten times a day. As far as classes were concerned, the days passed in a daze. Marnie made the supreme sacrifice and moved into my room so she could cue me on lines in the small hours of the morning. By Thursday, when I was conscious enough to notice, I thanked my stars that I seemed to be moving in a blanket of tolerance and compassion. Nobody bit back at me when I snapped. Celinda and Anne and Stella steered me through the day and then home to where Mama would be waiting in the hall with hot tea or soup. I snatched a nap before Kenneth arrived to walk me to rehearsals where we held onto each other for dear life. And no matter when rehearsals ended—at ten, or eleven, or after midnight—Pa would be sitting in the back of the auditorium, placidly puffing his pipe and marking papers as he waited to escort me home.

Pa, and my memory of his confidence, became my lifeline. We would walk home in silence through the soft dark night now growing warm with May, and my turbulent spirit could relax gratefully against his strength and faith. I don't know how I could have gotten through without it. Whenever I started getting panicky—say about once an hour—I would repeat to myself, "Pa knows I can do it," and feel my heart grow quiet.

Thursday's rehearsal, being the last, was the latest one of all. I was so tired my legs would scarcely march me home. When we reached our corner, I saw lights blazing. My heart lurched. "Mama's up. Pa, if she picks now to start a row. . . ."

"Don't count your chickens." Pa's mouth turned up at the corner as if he knew a secret. I walked into the house and there in the hall, purple suspenders, odoriferous pipe and all, stood Gramps!

"So much about your playactin' in your Ma's last letter, thought I'd better get on the train and come see the dadburned thing!"

"Not going to start talking about it now, Pa," Mama said firmly. She hustled me off to bed before I had a chance to say boo.

The next thing I knew, my room was bright with sunlight and Marnie was standing beside me with a cup of cocoa. "Mama says you're staying home today if she has to hog-tie you, and if the school doesn't like it they can tackle her. Gee, you look beat."

"Thanks a heap," I retorted.

"No, I mean it. You look awful pale."

My spirits revived. Evidently the bleaching cream was working, after all.

"I tried to persuade Mama to let me stay home and help you study lines, but she saw through the sacrifice." Marnie grinned. "I'll tell Celinda not to wait for you," she said, departing.

It was a weird sort of day. The hours ticked inexorably towards performance time. I wound my hair on rags and curled up on the bed for one last go over the potion scene. I went for a long walk around the neighborhood with Gramps, filling him in on play rehearsals. From the twinkle in his eye

I gathered my version differed considerably from Mama's. When we returned home, Mama reported that Bronwyn had called. "Said to tell you she got a book from the Library with the picture your costume's copied from. You go down there at five and she'll fix your hair to match it and give you supper." As soon as school got out, the girls piled in to find out why I'd stayed home and to fill me in on gossip. Mama chased them out again almost at once. "Child's got to get a nap before she leaves or she'll never last through performance!" The image of Mama as a stage mother tickled me no end.

I lay down obediently, but I couldn't sleep. Visions of play rehearsals were chasing themselves through my head, and my stomach was starting to do flip-flops. Downstairs I heard the front door open and close, and a deep rumble of voices. Pa had come home from school early as he'd promised, and brought Mr. Albright with him. Gramps's footsteps stomped in to join them in the study. Down in the kitchen pots and pans were clattering. Upstairs all was still. The whole household was revolving around me and my imminent debut, and the fact made me feel flattered but also awfully nervous. I wished the blasted clock would strike five so I could get out of here and have something to do to distract my mind.

When I couldn't stand it any longer, I slid out of bed and tiptoed cautiously out, hoping to look at the hall clock without getting caught by Mama. From the open study door came the sound of male laughter, and then Gramps's voice, which he never troubles to hush, no matter what. "Just how bad is this shindig tonight, Edward? Better tip me off so I'll be braced beforehand when things go wrong."

Pa laughed tolerantly. "I know amateur performances are awful, but if we've been living with it for two months you can stand it for a couple of hours. And remember, Cornelius, no matter what happens, not one of your cute comments afterwards. Don't even bat an eyelash. It will break Tish's heart if she ever finds out she's gotten into something over her head."

My hands had become glued to the stair railing. It wasn't Pa's words, it was the tone, the comfortable assumption in advance that I couldn't possibly be good. Pa sounded exactly the way I'd sound if I were discussing some little first-grade show of Missy's. My feet seemed to have suddenly sprouted lead weights and couldn't move. I clung there, shivering, hearing Gramps say, comfortably, "Ayuh, Tish always one for dramatizing, wasn't she? Comes of her wanting to be a writer, I suppose," and Mr. Albright's, "You have to give the youngsters credit for tackling Shakespeare at all. It wouldn't be fair to expect them to measure up to the play's standards."

And Pa—*laughing*—saying, "Don't know whether to laugh or cry over her sometimes. Must be wonderful to still have that innocence, to be able to believe if you want to do a thing badly enough you're bound to do it well." There was a rustle of paper, and Pa's voice started to read aloud my poem.

Et tu, Brute? I thought dully. My feet were able to move again, not fast, but they moved, in automatic silence, back to my room. The door shut quietly behind me. Like a wind-up toy I washed, and put on my best underwear under an old dress, and packed my small bag, and took the rags out of my hair. Then I went over and opened the window by the apple tree and peered cautiously out. I wasn't going to face the family's hypocrisy again today. I wasn't going to Bron, who was probably in on it too. I didn't know what I was going to do, other than get out of there fast. It had been years since I'd used the exit route of roof and tree, but I discovered that I hadn't lost the knack. When I stood at the bottom, panting, I ducked quickly out of sight behind the shrubbery and lit off down the block.

The numbness was wearing off, but the pain that followed it was worse. I was torn between wanting to run and hide, and wanting to *show* them, dammit, no matter what. My feet started running blindly, but I couldn't run from the fateful memory that followed me, or from my disillusionment, or from my fear, no matter where I went.

Finally I found myself standing on the corner by the church, the corner where I'd encountered Stella and Celinda, and without even being conscious of the decision, I knew what I had to do. I couldn't run away, I couldn't do that to Mr. Grimes, or Kenneth, or the school. I was going to have to go through with it to the best of my ability, with my head held high.

I turned and started towards the school, and Pa's words, Pa's tone, followed behind me like the Furies in the old Greek myths. I must have been wandering the streets for some time, for a lot of others had reached the school before me. Some must have spoken to me and received no answer, for I vaguely heard a murmur about "prima donna," but it scarcely registered. I went into the classroom designated as girls' dressing room, and started laying out the things I'd brought from home. Someone had already scattered stage make-up about, unfamiliar looking grease and burnt cork and rabbits' feet. I took off my dress and hung it up methodically, and started putting the cold cream on my face. Then I looked into the mirror at a stranger's face, hollow-eyed and haunted, and all at once I started to shake.

Anne's voice reached me. "Your costumes are hanging here in order, covered in sheets. I'm going to be your dresser, you know. Tish, can you hear me? What's wrong?"

I was shaking all over, the way Marnie had when she'd been so ill. Anne got me down into a chair, and I let my head drop down onto my arms on the hard table. I heard Anne's voice calling, and then Celinda and Stella were there, conferring in worried tones.

"What's the matter?"

"I don't know. Something big, or she'd never let go like this."

It felt weird to be discussed as if I weren't even there, but I didn't have the energy to protest. My teeth were chattering. Stella wrapped a shawl around my bare shoulders. "Want me to get Mr. Grimes?"

"*No!*" I took a deep breath and lied in my teeth. "I'm all right. Just nerves, I guess."

"Don't be silly," Stella said calmly. "You don't make fusses over nothing."

"You mean you don't think I'm that dramatic?" That was meant to be a joke, but it didn't come out quite the way I'd planned. Stella's eyes darkened with comprehension, and I found myself bawling. There were rustles around me—the room was filling up, and I knew that everyone was staring.

Celinda's arms went around me tightly. "Somebody go get Ken. Maybe he can find out what it's all about. C'mon, Tish, let's go someplace less public." She steered me out into the darkness of the cloakroom, and it suddenly struck me as terribly funny how many crises that cloakroom had witnessed during the past year, and I started to laugh and couldn't stop.

"Tish, stop it!" Celinda sounded scared.

Somebody tall loomed up beside me. It was Kenneth, already in his first scene costume. I flung myself against his beautiful blue velvet tunic and just let go.

Ken held me and let me bawl a few minutes, then produced a handkerchief and wiped my eyes. A lot of cold cream came off along with the tears and that made me laugh again.

"I'm glad you haven't lost your sense of humor," Ken said

grimly. "Tish, what's happened? Are you sick? If you can't go on, you've got to let Mr. Grimes know fast."

I backed off a little and looked at him, really looked for a change, and was shocked to see how tired and tense he looked. And it finally dawned on me that Ken, as Romeo, was under just as heavy a burden of responsibility as I, and I didn't have any business doing this to him just before he went onstage.

I took a deep breath and set myself to the biggest acting job of my life. "Ken, I'll be all right. Honest. It's—just nerves and being overtired." To my inordinate relief my voice sounded halfway normal. "I promise you, I'm not going to go to pieces again and let you down."

I was proud that I was able to smile at him without my chin shaking, to walk back into the dressing room and sit down before the mirror with a measure of calm. But I couldn't manage to get the two sides of my face to match. Stella took the brushes and colors from my hands. "I'll do that," she said matter-of-factly, and proceeded to finish making up my face. Celinda closed my fingers around a cup of tea, which she'd managed by some miracle to produce. The steaming heat felt good. Anne calmly started to fix my hair.

Vaguely I was aware that the dressing room was crowded now, that tension was accelerating as curtain time drew near, that I was surrounded by whispers and speculation. But it was all held off from me by a little circle of concern. Within it, not even the reality of opening night registered on me. I was numb, like you are in that split second after you've cut yourself but before the pain has hit.

At last my mother hens had me put together to their satisfaction, and they marched me into the wings like a dressed-up doll. "Stay here. Don't move. We'll explain to Mr. Grimes." Celinda gave me a quick kiss for luck. "I'm going out front now. Larry Molloy's saving seats for Stel and me in the front row. We'll be back here the minute the play is over." Our friends and relations had been given stern orders not to venture backstage during intermissions.

"But I'll be here," Anne said. "I'll have your costumes right here in the wings so you can make quick changes. I'm going to get them now." She and Celinda vanished, and I was left with Stella, who took both my hands and held them tightly.

"Tish," she said rapidly, "I don't know what's wrong, and cross my heart and hope to die, I'm not trying to play God. But I want to tell you something Malenkaia used to say to me. She's Mama's grandmother, and she's awfully Russian. Whenever we kids used to be up against something we thought we couldn't do, because it was too big or something dreadful had happened, she used to tell us the story of Jacob wrestling with the angel. She used to say the moral was, 'Don't fight it, *use* it.' I know you can do it, Tish. I saw you at tryouts, remember?" She hugged me hard, and was gone, and I was alone in the dusty blackness where Ken and I had spent so many hours together during the past months.

I wished Ken was with me, but his first entrance was made from the other side of the stage. From beyond the velvet curtains came the rustle of the audience, and the opening notes of the high school orchestra playing the overture. My palms felt clammy and my legs were becoming the consistency of melting jelly. I wished Stella was still there to talk me into Juliet, the way she'd done at tryouts. I was surrounded by people, and by love and concern—even from my family who despite everything were hoping for the best—but I was nonetheless alone. *Don't fight it, use it,* I thought, and it suddenly hit me that this must have been the way Juliet had felt, especially when she was being forced to marry Paris. This must be the disillusion she'd felt towards her parents, whom she'd tried to please; towards the nurse, in whose support she'd thought that she could trust. This numbness was what Juliet must have felt when she had stabbed herself. I felt as if I were looking at a puzzle in which for the first time all the pieces were falling into place.

In another moment Lady Capulet was calling, "Nurse, where's my daughter? Call her forth to me," and I was running onto the stage.

The tempo accelerated, time tumbled over itself as Romeo and Juliet's too-young love rushed them to their doom in the still Verona heat. The potion scene was approaching; it was past; now it was the tomb scene with the apparitions frighteningly real. Then it was over, and I was lying crumbled over the bier, my head spilling over the edge down onto Kenneth's shoulder. Beside us tall tapers glowed.

> For never was a tale more full of woe,
> Than this of Juliet and her Romeo.

There was a silence, then a muffled roar of applause, like waves lapping the shores of a distant sea. The curtains closed. The curtains opened. We took bows dazedly. Someone thrust a bouquet into my arms. From my family, probably. I didn't want to look at it now. At last, blessedly, the curtains closed for good, and Kenneth grabbed my hand, and we stumbled together into our secret backstage place, and clung together like two kids who had just emerged together out of a nightmare to a mountaintop. We didn't know whether we were in Verona or West Farms.

"Oh, wow," Ken said at last, releasing me. "We made it. Oh, wow, Tish."

"I know."

Celinda and Stella groped their way through the dark clutter to us. They'd both been crying. They didn't say anything, just hugged me hard. Then we all looked at each other and started laughing, like a dam bursting.

"You did it. You really did it! Sourpuss Sadie had a tear in her eye. I do not lie," Stella said solemnly. "Tish, your family's waiting out in the hall. They're really stunned. Your mother's speechless, and your father's jaw has dropped two notches."

The fragile mood was shattered. I turned away. "I don't want to see them. Not now. Ken, will you take me home?"

"Why—yeah. Sure. For Pete's sake, what's wrong?"

As usual I didn't have the sense to keep my mouth shut. "They thought I'd make a fool of myself and disgrace them. They darn near made me do it. I'm not in the mood for their congratulations now."

There was a silence. "'For each man kills the thing he loves,'" Ken murmured.

"*What?*"

"Nothing. Just something I read somewhere."

"I'll go do something." Stella started out, then turned. "Tish, are you quite sure *you're* not trying to be God?"

"Oh, hell and damn! Why does everything have to ruin the play for me!" I burst out and, in tiredness, shame, and anger, proceeded to make a fool of myself by starting to cry.

It was an uncomfortable moment for all concerned, broken at last by familiar determined footsteps. "Clear out, all of you. Child's dead exhausted and I'm takin' her home directly." Before I could protest, Gramps had scooped me up, costume and all, and marched with me out to the empty carriage.

"Sidney's bringing the others. Figgered mebbe you needed time alone to descend to earth." Gramps's brow beetled. "Now would you mind telling me why in tarnation you scared the wits out of us by skinning out like that? Your Ma was nervous as a June bug till it occurred to her to call the school."

"I don't want to talk about it."

"All right," Gramps said mildly. "Then let's talk about the play. Danged good. Jolted your Ma a piece, and that old Kate, too. We're right proud of you."

"Ha," I said bitterly.

Gramps frowned again, then his forehead cleared and he struck his knee. "You weren't by any chance hanging around the study door this afternoon? That why you lit out? All right, so mebbe we did underestimate you, but goldurn it, girl, don't it give you any satisfaction to prove us wrong?"

"I thought Pa had faith in my—my creative abilities. I always thought *he* believed in me, no matter what."

Gramps was silent for a moment. "All right, you had a shock. I'm not denying it. But I thought you'd gotten used to the notion parents were human beings with feet of clay. I recollect you making a few profound statements as to how becoming grown-up was worth the pain."

"That's not the point," I said with dignity. "I just can't go back to feeling the same way I did before I—lost my illusions."

"Whoever said you could?" Gramps demanded. "You ever read Wordsworth, Tish?" He straightened, cleared his throat impressively and quoted:

> *Though nothing can bring back the hour*
> *Of splendour in the grass, of glory in the flower;*
> *We will grieve not, rather find*
> *Strength in what remains behind.*

"Tish, are you sure you're crying because of something your father's done, or because you're mad that you can't run back to Eden?"

We reached home, and I ran inside in silence while he drove around to the barn to unhitch. By hustling, I was able to get my face paint off and to be in bed with the light out when the family arrived. I could hear their muted laughter, and murmurs of approbation, as they tiptoed around trying not to wake me. But tired as I was, I was not near to sleep. I stared at the ceiling, trying to relive the play, while instead a lot of things that had been said to me, which I'd have preferred not to think about, ran through my head.

I had expected the day to be a Keeping Day. But a Keeping Day was supposed to be a memory you wanted to hold onto. Today was a memory that was going to hold onto me.

CHAPTER NINE

May

It was quite a shock coming down to earth again after *Romeo and Juliet* was over.

The second night the auditorium was packed, for news of our triumph had spread. It was a sweltering night, especially for the actors in our heavy costumes, but the audience didn't seem to mind. It howled with delight, it cried, it stamped and clapped. There was a party at Lady Capulet's afterwards for all of the Browning Society, the cast, and the crew. We gave Mr. Grimes a framed etching of William Shakespeare, and he responded with a witty and moving speech.

I fully expected to be off on a crying jag at that point, but as it turned out I had neither the energy nor the awareness to be maudlin, for I was starting to develop chills and fever. The room started going around and then went black, and the next thing I knew Ken had telephoned Pa to come and get me, and then Mama was bundling me off to bed and muttering, "Small wonder! Life you've been leading lately!"

Mama made me stay home from school two days. At first I luxuriated in the freedom and the fuss my friends made over me when they dropped by after school. But by Wednesday, when Mama finally let me out, I was itching to get back into things—and besides, let's face it, I was no end riled to be missing the school's first astonishment at my performance. Schools, as I well knew, forget sensations fast.

Getting back to normal life was like surfacing after a long period underwater. Everything seemed to have changed without my noticing. May was well begun, days were growing hot, and spring fever had reached epidemic proportions, with teachers running themselves ragged trying to overcome it. By the end of the week I was ready to jump out of my skin from boredom, not having the tension and excitement of rehearsals to look forward to.

I turned to my writing, neglected for some time, and wrote a story of a girl being in a play and how it changed her life. Writing it made me cry, but on reading it over even I had the sense to see it was oversentimental. I wrote another story about my encounter with Mary Lou in the cloakroom, and this turned out far better, although I knew I must never dare show it to a soul. I wondered what was happening with Mary Lou. She looked like death warmed over. Doug, his protection of the play removed, had promptly gotten bounced out on suspension for a week, and it was sheer luck that Ben escaped the same fate.

Everyone, it seemed, was restless. We needed something to plan for, something to look forward to. I settled to the task of retrieving my dwindling grades, and to mending the rickety bridges of my social relationships. I knew darn well I never would have made it through the play without the help of my friends. They'd been angels of tolerance, and it was high time I showed them I was grateful. What I would have liked to do was throw a party, but since my birthday celebration was coming up in another month, and I was determined this year it was going to be a glamorous evening affair, I didn't want to push my luck with Mama. So I contented myself with having kids over for supper, going downtown shopping with the girls on Saturday, spending afternoons sewing or at the Library with Celinda, helping those I could with homework.

I got back into Mama's good graces by taking Missy and Katie over to the pond to play on sunny afternoons. Stella would come, too, bringing her little brother, and Anne with her sketch pad and Cee with her needlework. We discovered we could liven up our homework reading assignments if one of us read aloud while the others listened. But most of the time we'd spend in the lazy drifting I hadn't had time for lately, and I'd find myself wishing myself back in rehearsals in the dark backstage intimacy with Ken.

Maybe it was just as well that the play was over. *Romeo and Juliet* had taught us a pattern of intimacy, of touching and of being in each other's arms, that was hard to break, but which definitely did not fit into our outside world. More than once I intercepted significant looks from teachers when I automatically tucked my hand through his arm as we walked to classes. It made me feel self-conscious with him, which I didn't like. I suspected Kenneth was feeling the same way.

Ken was helping out afternoons at his father's store, and it was hard to get used to seeing him only in English, or in the few minutes between our other classes, and at church on Sunday. Already I was getting scared about what would happen over the summer if Ken went back to Pennsylvania, and I could understand how Mary Lou apparently was still feeling over Doug. So I was overjoyed when Stella telephoned breathlessly one afternoon. "Come up right away, can you? And bring Celinda. Mama just gave in about letting me have a big birthday party next weekend, so let's make plans fast before she recovers her senses!"

When Celinda and I got there, we found Anne and Stella

already installed on the Molloys' side porch with a pitcher of iced tea and a plate of honey nut cake, Stella's specialty. "I've been buttering Ma up to make her melt," Stella said, referring to the cake and the fact that she was minding Timmy, who crawled happily about under everybody's feet. Stella was chewing on a pencil end and had put on her managing face.

"Who shall we have? While Mama's being weak-minded we might as well ask as many as the house can hold. All our crowd from lunch, of course, and Ben, and the Lathams. Junius. Jimmy Breidenbach." Stella looked at me. "Would your mother let Marnie come? She's practically in high school now, for goodness sake."

"Won't hurt to ask. Marnie'd be thrilled. And she's in Mama's good graces just now since she did so many of my chores while the play was on."

"Mary Lou?" Anne asked.

Stella grimaced. "I suppose I have to. By the way, Tish, Mama's in a swivet because your Aunt Kate told her wild tales about a party Mary Lou had last year. So this is going to be a Scavenger Party. We're sending people out with lists, and a time limit, so they won't have a chance to get lost in the bushes and spoon."

"Mary Lou'll manage anyway," I said waspishly.

Stella laughed. "She must be getting desperate. She even tried her wiles on my brother the other day."

"What did Larry do?"

"Looked at her as if she were some strange creature who'd intruded under his microscope lens, and walked away. Larry doesn't know much about women, but he has that much sense. Poor Mary Lou, she must have really worn out the list of eligibles if she's down to Larry."

Celinda looked up innocently. "He's not that bad."

"He's not bad at all. He's a brilliant dedicated scientist, but he's girl-shy." Stella's eyes twinkled. "All right, Celinda, that settles one problem. I'll put you down as Larry's partner. I'm pairing everybody up in couples for the Scavenger Hunt. And we need some more cute boys, so think of some, somebody, quick!"

Celinda, who'd been looking more and more alarmed, stood up hastily. "I don't know whether I'll be able to come. You'd better not count on it. I have to go home now and start supper." She beat a rapid exit, accompanied by Anne, whose mother had started to holler for her down the street.

Stella looked at me in astonishment. "What happened to *her?*"

"You mentioned couples. Celinda's scared of boys. Haven't you ever noticed?"

"But that's ridiculous. Celinda's a pretty girl. Or would be," Stella added practically, "if she'd just let go more. We'd better try to fix her up with someone."

"It's been tried." I hesitated, feeling like a traitor. But Stella had become a very good friend—and besides, she had the deductive instincts of a Sherlock Holmes. She'd find out anyway, and it might as well be straight from me. "You weren't at the dance down at my church. Bron and I—well, we blackmailed Cee and Junius into going together."

I stopped, remembering, while Stella waited. "It was awful. You remember what Celinda's mother's like." Stella nodded. "She marched in and dragged Cee out. Everybody saw what happened after that. But you couldn't see what happened inside. That sick old crow's convinced Celinda that having anything to do with the opposite sex is awful and dirty. And that prize chicken, my sister's stepson, did not exactly behave like Sir Galahad himself."

"Oh," Stella said softly. "Well. I think I'll put Larry with her anyway. I have to team him with someone, and he wouldn't hurt a fly. Who do you think your brother wants to be paired with?"

"I don't think he much cares." There had been an odd note in Stella's voice that made my ears perk up. Stella wasn't looking at me, which was unusual; she was doodling very busily in her notebook. It dawned on me that Ben had been spending a lot of time around Molloys' house lately, exploring scientific experiments and philosophic discussions with her brother. "Why?" I asked, as if I wasn't beginning to know.

"I was just wondering. So I'd know who to put him with, that's all." Stella's face had turned pink. "Tish," she said irrelevantly, "is Ben in trouble in school again? Lately, when he's been around with Larry, he's seemed so—I don't know, *down*."

"You noticed it, too? He's had his walls up a mile high around home. I guess I was too wrapped up in myself to notice it till the play was over." Stella and I looked at each other. "I think he's worried about Doug. Doug got kicked out again yesterday. He got caught setting off a firecracker in the Boys' Room. Ken says Mr. Moore told him one more charge against him, for anything, and he'd be expelled for good. Ben's been his best friend since they were Missy's age, and I guess he's worried."

"Doug's changed," Stella said thoughtfully. "Just since I've known him, even. Last fall he was—oh, I don't know, wild, but he was still fun. Now he scares me. Sometimes I even feel sorry for poor old Mary Lou. She's still crazy about him. And it's embarrassing."

You don't know the half of it, I thought.

After this illuminating conversation, I made it my business

to keep my eyes peeled where these various friends and relations were concerned. I was right, I decided, intrigued, in thinking Stella was developing a crush on Ben. Stella, the self-sufficient and the self-controlled! For the life of me I couldn't see what the attraction was, other than the fact that they were both bright, and shrewd, and didn't care what people thought. Then I remembered that a year before I hadn't thought Kenneth worth noticing either. It hardly seemed possible.

Stella and her matter-of-fact compassion would be good for Ben. But there was fat chance he'd get around to noticing. He was definitely in one of his Heathcliff moods, and Doug Latham seemed the only explanation. At least Ben hadn't been involved in the firecracker episode, or in Doug's most recent incident of playing hooky.

The Lathams, too, were worried about Doug, Ken confided as we walked together on the way to Stella's party. Naturally we were supposed to be going in a bunch, Ben and Marnie and I and Ken and Jimmy. But as soon as we were out of range of Aunt Kate's spyglass, Ben stalked ahead, wrapped in his black silence, and Marnie and Jimmy galloped around acting like Cicero does when he thinks he's still a puppy. Marnie had submitted to being dolled up like a lady, but she wasn't letting it cramp her style. Ken and I loitered, bringing up the rear. We had little chance these days for private talk, for you couldn't discuss family matters in the corridors at school.

There'd been a showdown at home over the firecracker episode, Ken told me. Mr. Moore had sent for both Mr. and Mrs. Latham to come to school to collect Doug for his suspension. Mr. Latham had not appreciated being called away from the feed and grain store. "They had a row that night, a big one. Doug actually swung at Pa! For a minute I thought my father was going to put him through the wall. But he didn't, of course. He never does." Ken's eyes were troubled. "Sometimes I get scared wondering what's going to happen next."

I remembered what Stella had said about feeling afraid of Doug at times.

We reached the Molloy house and there was no chance for further talk. Stella hadn't been fooling when she said the party was going to be big. Lights, noise, and laughter poured from every corner of the big old house. Even the little kids, who'd been put to bed, were hanging over the bannisters enjoying the fun. Celinda was looking panicky, but she was there.

"Remember that afternoon in the churchyard? I told her if she didn't come, I'd *know* I was right in thinking I wasn't wanted," Stella whispered. "And it worked. I did put her with Larry, too."

Mrs. Molloy was dividing the mob into couples and handing out the lists. These were greeted by elaborate groans. "No loitering now," she said firmly, but her eyes were twinkling. "You can go anywhere in a ten-block square. You have exactly an hour. The first couple back with the most complete list wins the prize!"

In the uproar, Mary Lou barged over to grab Stella's arm. "I don't care how you do it, but you've got to put me with Doug. Please! I've got to talk to him, and he keeps avoiding me."

"Oh, for goodness sake!" Stella exclaimed. "Everything's all arranged. It'll mess up everything." She looked at Mary Lou's eyes and relented. "I'll try. But I can't promise. He might still bolt, you know."

But when we finally started out, Mary Lou was hanging firmly to Doug's arm. He looked like a thundercloud. It might have messed up a lot of arrangements, but I noticed Stella still managed to end up with Ben herself. Ken came to claim me.

"I'm glad to see Stella had some sense," he said, grinning.

Out under the streetlight we paused to peruse the list. Mr. Molloy had made it up, and it was a holy terror. "A newspaper headline on the outbreak of the Spanish-American War! Where are we supposed to find that?"

"Up in our attic, if Ben didn't manage to burn it up. Pa never throws away things like that. Come on!" And we were off.

Within three-quarters of an hour we were exhausted, half-frustrated and half-triumphant, and the possessors of all items but three. We were also flushed and dusty, having been through attics and cellars of his house, mine, Bron's, and even Aunt Kate's, one place we figured no one else would have the nerve to try.

We stopped, breathless, under the streetlight by Molloys', and looked at each other. "We're never going to find those last three, and I don't care," Ken said. "I also don't care if Stella's mother does get mad. We never get to see each other any more." He held out his hand, and I took it, and we tiptoed around the house into the solitude behind the lilac thicket out back. There in the fragrant darkness we knelt down facing each other, our knees just touching, as we'd done so often in the backstage shadows. We smiled at each other, and my heart started to pound.

"Gee, this feels good again," Ken said. "I never get to see you any more. I didn't know how much I'd missed it."

"Me, either," I said. "I wish the play had never had to be over."

"You were good, you know," Ken said with such detached consideration that I almost laughed. "I never got to tell you so that night. You were really good."

"So were you."

"Maybe," Ken said, "it was because it really wasn't acting."

In the shimmering silence a soft breeze riffled the lilacs showering us with fragrance. Slowly, his hands still at his sides, Ken leaned forward and kissed me the way he had done it in the play. And it wasn't playacting, any more than it had been then. It was gentle, and tender, and not at all the brutal way Herbie had kissed me in the pantry, but my body was responding the same way it had then. Our hands weren't at our sides any more. When we broke apart, we sat back shaken, staring at each other.

"I think," Kenneth said slowly, "that I'm in love with you."

At that shattering moment, what should come crashing by outside the lilac bushes but the unmistakable noisy footsteps of Jimmy Breidenbach and my sister Marnie. I ducked away, my face scarlet. Ken jumped to his feet. "Come on," he mumbled, "We'd better get inside!"

We stumbled, blinking, into the bright lights of the crowded parlor. There were lilac petals clinging to my rumpled skirts. I wondered if my face betrayed what was going on inside.

Everybody seemed to be back now. Mr. Molloy was calling "Time!" and collecting our bags of loot. Stella looked around. "We're all here but Doug and Mary Lou. Anybody seen them?"

"Jimmy and I passed them by the park half an hour ago," Marnie said. "They were having an awful row. And she was crying. I'll bet she ran back home."

"We shan't wait for them," Mrs. Molloy said smoothly. "Who got back first? Celinda and Larry? Unpack your things, and Mr. Molloy will check them off." Pair by pair we hauled out our finds, amid jeers and roars. The biggest howl was when Jimmy Breidenbach produced his mother's old corset for the "container to hold 150 lbs." Stella and Ben were tied with us for three items missing. But to everyone's surprise the winners were Larry and Celinda, who had located everything except a hoopskirt.

"Guess our minds just work well together," Larry said, unruffled. Stella's eyes met mine with mirthful triumph.

We all trooped into the dining room for platters of sandwiches, and punch, and ice cream and cake. Stella opened her presents—she handled that chore with considerably more poise than I usually managed. Afterwards Mrs. Molloy let us dance for half an hour before she threw everybody out. The three Sterlings and Jimmy and Kenneth and Celinda stayed to help Stella and Larry do the dishes, and that was the most fun of all. Ben seemed to have shaken off his black mood for a while, and I have never seen Larry loosen up so much. It was probably because he felt at home with Ben. We got to talking about the picnics we used to go on as kids.

"Why don't we go on one next Saturday?" Larry suggested. "Go over to Staten Island on the ferry. There's some interesting marine life along the shore I've been wanting to examine. How about it, Ben? You and Stella, and Ken and Tish. And Jimmy and Marnie if they can stand being serious long enough for me to collect some good specimens."

Stella poked me. "How about Celinda?" she demanded.

"Oh, Celinda's coming with me," Larry said matter-of-factly. "She's the first female I've ever met who's had the good sense not to try to make me over."

Well! Stella and I managed to avoid looking at each other. Neither of us dared cast a glance in Cee's direction. But she definitely, I noticed, did not run away.

I had a lot to think about before I fell asleep that night.

I never did manage to find out what had happened to Doug and Mary Lou. Neither had Ken, I learned when we compared notes after church. "Doug didn't get in till hours after I did," he reported. "I heard him sneaking in around three a.m. And he lit out again first thing this morning." Mary Lou was not in church, which was not particularly unusual. Neither one of them showed up at Young People's that night. Mary Lou wasn't in school Monday or Tuesday, either, although Doug was—apparently Mr. Moore's latest ultimatum had gotten through. After school I saw Ben and Doug going off together, but when I tried to pump Ben about it at suppertime he just told me irritably to mind my own business.

Stella and I were agog to know what was going on in Celinda's little head, but Cee had pulled her wall of calm reserve around her. After school that week, whenever Celinda wasn't with us, Stella and I discussed and speculated. "Larry's as bad as she is," Stella complained. "A regular clam!"

I was relieved that Stella was wrapped up in the mystery of Larry and Celinda, because it kept her from concentrating on me. I knew her sharp eyes had spotted the crumpled lilacs on my skirt that night, and I definitely did not want to discuss the subject. As a matter of fact, I even felt self-conscious around Kenneth, when we walked to class together.

A lively correspondence in notes was passed back and forth all week as we planned the picnic. Mr. Grimes, who intercepted one of these missives on Friday morning, looked amused. He was more easygoing now that the play was over. "Thank goodness he got one of the tame ones," Stella murmured to me at lunch. "I almost died thinking it was the one I'd written you about Mary Lou."

"I saw her in the hall this morning. You're right, she does look awful."

"I guess she finally got the message from Doug on Saturday," Stella said. "This is one time I can't much blame him for acting like a rat. She does cling so!"

"Here comes la belle Hodge now," I said. "I was hoping maybe she'd do us a favor today and go home. Gee, she looks sick."

Mary Lou really did. But it hadn't affected her disposition any. She sat down among us with her usual sweet comments. In the next seat her bosom pal, Charlene, started unwrapping sardine sandwiches. "Phew," Stella whispered. "On a hot day like this." Then, "What's the matter with Mary Lou? *Quick!*"

I jumped. Mary Lou's face had turned pale green and without a word she slid out of her chair and down onto the floor like a limp rag doll. Everybody just stared stupidly, including Charlene with a half-chewed chunk of sandwich stuffed in her silly face. Stella and I dove under the table and came up on either side of Mary Lou, who did look decidedly sick and kind of pathetic. "Anybody got smelling salts?" I asked.

Everybody milled around but nothing was accomplished. I was rubbing Mary Lou's hands. "I'll get someone to carry her to the nurse." Stella dashed off and returned with Ben, who surveyed the patient with some distaste, scooped her up, and marched off with Stella and me trailing after. I guess we both figured we owed a favor to Mary Lou.

To our relief the nurse took over and dismissed us, and by that time lunch period was past and it was time for our first afternoon class. Through the window I saw a hack arrive to deliver Mary Lou back home.

"I wonder what happened," I said to Stella after school, when she and Celinda came over to finish last-minute plans for the picnic menu. We filled Mama in on all the details while she iced us a chocolate cake.

"I think she's been dieting," Stella said. "Haven't you noticed how thin she's gotten? She doesn't have a good shape any more. You can see her collarbones."

Mama snorted. "Child never has known how to look after

herself properly. Not brought up right. Grace Hodge never has had any sense."

I was up with the birds on Saturday to pack our picnic basket. The plan was for everyone to congregate at our house at eight and leave from there. Eight o'clock came, and Jimmy Breidenbach arrived from next door, and he and Marnie went out and started playing ball, but there was no sign of the others. At eight-thirty Celinda telephoned.

"Is anything wrong? Stella and Larry were going to stop for me on their way down, and they haven't come."

"Ken's not here either." I felt a prick of worry. "It does seem funny."

"Get off the line, and I'll call Larry," Ben ordered. "Women!" he muttered as he cranked the phone. "Always talking about something instead of getting to the bottom of it. Larry? Where is everyone?"

We heard the rumble of a voice at the other end of the wire, and then Ben hung up, looking puzzled. "The picnic's postponed till next week. He didn't explain. Says something's happening at Hodges', and Stella had to go over to help."

I looked at him, bewildered. "Well—it was nice of them to let us know."

"I'm going over to the park—see if I can find some fellows to hit a ball around." Ben departed before Mama could dream him up a job.

Mama was already hollering the message out to Jimmy and Marnie, and they too were about to take off, only this time Mama and Mrs. Breidenbach nailed them first. I telephoned Celinda, who accepted the message fatalistically. Mama put the coffeepot on the stove to hotten up. Pa poured himself some and took it into the study to commune with his shorthand papers.

The telephone rang and I jumped, hoping it was Ken. But it was only Aunt Kate, seeking someone sacrificial enough to plant her wagonload of new perennials. Since Ben was missing and Marnie assigned the mopping and dusting, guess who was left.

"Time enough yet. Don't have to rush. Sit down and I'll cook a proper breakfast. Haven't been eating enough lately." Mama began to rattle pots and pans briskly. I sat down in the rocker by the fire and started rocking Katie's cradle with my toe. Katie, who's happy over any attention offered, started to coo.

The telephone rang again, and it *was* Ken. He sounded strange. "I'm sorry about the picnic. I can't explain now," he said and actually hung up on me.

I dropped the receiver slowly and turned to Mama, feeling queer. "He wouldn't even explain!"

"Will when he's ready, and you know it," Mama said comfortably, taking nut bread from the oven. "Probably something to do with that fool brother."

The smell of nut bread quickly attracted Marnie and the little kids. Missy proudly carried a plate of it in to Pa, and the rest of us settled around the kitchen table and had a real cozy time. Finally Mama pushed back her chair. "Getting lazy, sitting round like this. Work to do, drat it."

"I suppose," I said, "I'd better go plant those flowers for Aunt Kate."

"Suppose you had." Mama's eyes twinkled. "Foot in mouth disease. Runs in the family, don't it?"

"Not with me," Marnie said with misplaced virtue. "At least not when it comes to making Aunt K fool promises. That dumb I'm not." She looked out the window. "For Pete's sake, here comes Stella. What's got into *her*?"

Stella burst into our kitchen without even stopping to knock. "Mrs. Sterling, Mama says—can you come, right now. . . ." She was so painfully out of breath she hung on the door frame for support, and her eyes were awful. "You're a friend of Mrs. Hodge's, aren't you?"

"Know her from church, acourse. Neighbors. What's the matter?"

"It's Mary Lou." Stella dropped limply into a chair. "She got an overdose of medicine. She's all right now," she added hastily as Mama jumped up. "At least, she's out of danger. But Mrs. Hodge doesn't want the doctor told. Mama thought maybe you could talk sense into her."

Mama was already pinning on her hat and grabbing her bag. "Take care of the young ones," she flung behind her as she dashed off. Stella had jumped up and was pacing in nervous energy, as if unsure whether to laugh or cry or have the shakes. Marnie handed her a glass of milk. I pushed her down again into the chair.

"Sit down and drink that. Stel, what happened?"

"I guess I might as well tell you. It will be all over town by night." Stella's glance flicked at Missy, openmouthed in the doorway. "Can't we go someplace private?"

"Up to my room, if you don't mind the bed not made."

"That's the last thing," Stella said, "that matters." She climbed the stairs doggedly, while behind her back Marnie and I exchanged alarmed and puzzled glances.

Once in my room, I shut the door and locked it firmly. Then my eyes widened. "Stella, are you all right?" Stella, the calm, the self-controlled, had started to shake all over as if she had the chill. Suddenly, with a choked sob, she threw herself face-down in my rumpled pillow.

"Want me to butt out?" Marnie asked with unaccustomed delicacy.

Stella sat up, face averted, and shook her head. "I guess I've been holding it in too long, something had to give. Oh, girls, Mary Lou tried to kill herself."

"You're joking!"

"I wish I were," Stella said soberly. "She wrote a note. I saw it. She drank a whole bottle of laudanum. That's thirty-three grains of opium per ounce." Trust Stella to know a thing like that. We looked at each other in silence.

"She's been in a rotten mood for weeks," Stella said finally. "And awfully unhappy. Everybody knew that." *But nobody did anything about it,* both of us were thinking.

"I may have a dirty mind, but is she getting a baby?" Marnie has a terrifying flair for voicing what others are trying not to think. Stella nodded slowly.

"Doug, of course."

"And he's run away. It must have just finished Mary Lou. No wonder she—" Stella pressed one hand hard against her chin and hugged herself as if to hold herself together.

"How—did it happen?" I finally thought to ask. "And how did you get mixed in?"

"Her mother found her this morning and started yelling. Mama was out on the back porch and heard, so we ran right over." Stella was silent for a minute. "Isn't it just like Mary Lou not to do anything right, not even commit suicide? She must've been up half the night, and we found her at six, so the laudanum hadn't had time to more than drug her. She was barely breathing, though. And Mrs. Hodge was bound and determined not to call the doctor. Just kept wringing her hands and hollering about the disgrace!" Stella said bitterly. "I swear to God, I think she'd have seen her die first!"

I couldn't speak. Stella went and stood by the window, looking up the street. "Well," she said flatly, "she'll survive, I guess, thanks to my mother. I never knew Mama knew so many ways to make people sick. We kept forcing mustard and soapsuds and black coffee in her till there couldn't possibly be any laudanum left, and in between we took turns walking her up and down so she couldn't fall asleep." Stella rubbed her shoulders. "I must have walked a thousand miles with Mary Lou a dead weight on my neck. And every inch of it remembering every mean thing I ever said about her."

"All of them probably true," Marnie said quietly.

Stella looked at her. "Maybe that makes it worse."

None of us knew what to say. We just sat around in silence, full of thoughts. Suddenly Stella banged her hand down hard on the bureau. "It's all so rotten!"

"What is?"

"I don't know. Everything. Life. That things like this can happen." Stella turned to me, the tears beginning to trickle down her cheeks. "That poor kid. For the first time in my life I really felt sorry for her. And there wasn't a thing that I could do."

"You did plenty."

Stella went on heedlessly. "We didn't even have the decency to let her decide for herself whether to live or die. Maybe Mary Lou was right. What's ahead for her now? Doug's gone."

"He's no loss. And he's too young to get married."

"By night the whole neighborhood'll know, no matter how her mother tries to hush it up. It's exactly what the old cats have been expecting of the Hodges! They'll never let her forget it, all her life."

"You're wrong," I said positively. "It'll be a ten days' wonder. And everybody'll remember when the baby first comes. But I bet you a nickel Mrs. Hodge tries to pass it off as hers. And everybody'll know, but nobody'll say." Half-remembered stories I'd absorbed in childhood drifted back to mind. "It's happened that way before. Within five years everybody'll have forgotten. Because things like this can't be allowed to have happened in our nice neighborhood. Nobody could take it. So, nobody'll remember—except Mary Lou herself."

"Dear God," Stella said slowly.

"Come on," I said, "we'd better go down and fix the little kids some lunch."

We wandered downstairs, feeling kind of lost. Peter had departed to his own devices but Missy had improved the shining hour by embarking on her own idea of making cookies, which meant the kitchen was a mess.

Marnie looked and laughed ruefully. "It doesn't even seem worth yelling about today." She swept up the flour while I tried to get the eggs off the floor. Stella attended to Katie, who was being good-natured about her dire need for a dry diaper.

"Doesn't seem fair for you to come to our house and do a job like that."

"I don't mind. I've had lots of practice." Stella looked at me. "Would you mind if I stayed around today? I just don't feel like going home."

So Stella stayed and helped make a fresh batch of cookies to replace Missy's disastrous attempt. The rest of the family came drifting in, all but Pa, who'd gone down to the school to work. Mama came in when we were just finished eating lunch and sat down wearily. She looked angry, as she always did when she was deeply moved. "Girl'll pull through. Don't know about her family. Doctor came and gave Grace Hodge some syrup, which shut *her* up. Fool woman's been wailing all morning about how could the child do this to her! Last thing she needs to hear!"

"Mama, is Mary Lou? . . ."

Mama's eyes flicked warningly towards Missy, but she nodded. "Yep. Viney's with her now. Brought Viney up short, I can tell you. A wonder it didn't happen to her. Both those girls been headed down that road for years. Seems like there must have been something one of us could have done to stop them." Mama was silent a minute. "Poor Emma Jane Latham. Wonder if it'd be tactful for me to stop by later. Mr. Hodge was there last night, raising holy hell."

It hadn't occurred to me before how this would affect the Lathams.

Ben pushed back his chair. "I'm going over there. See if I can do anything. Doug's my friend, after all!" He said it fiercely, as if expecting an argument, which he didn't get, and bolted out. Stella looked after him somberly. Mama, for no apparent reason, grabbed up Katie and hugged her hard.

Marnie went across the way and silently started planting Aunt Kate's perennials. Stella and I followed, and we worked in silence. Somehow I felt better having something to do. The hot sun felt like summer, and up in the apple tree a bird was singing. After a while I saw Mama come out, dressed for calling, and head towards Lathams'. Shortly after, Ben hurdled the back fence. He'd taken the back way through the yards, and he was out of breath.

"Tish, you'd better go find Ken. The vultures have been gathering—Aunt Kate and Miss Albright are there already—and he's cut out. This has hit him hard."

I didn't stop to clean myself up or excuse myself to Stella. I just cut out as fast I could run. I knew without thinking where to go, to our secret place in the back of the empty lot. At this time of year it was overgrown waist-deep in flowers and wild grasses, like Gramps's fields. Beyond it great trees rose like a forest of dark shadows. I saw Kenneth, his shoulders heaving, leaning his head on his arm against a copper beech. And I waded into the waist-deep sea.

"Kenneth!" I called, and held out my arms. Kenneth turned. He'd been crying. He stared at me for a second while life and death hung in the balance. Then he was running, stumbling towards me through a rippling sea of grass. He ran at me so hard that when he came into my arms I lost my balance and we went down in a tangle of clothes and flowers and wild sweet grasses. Ken was crying, his face buried between my breasts as if he wanted to burrow inside my body like a desperate child. He was holding me so tight I couldn't breathe, and a sharp rock dug painfully into my shoulders, but I didn't move. I wouldn't have moved to save my soul.

Presently, with a muffled oath, he released me and jumped up. He stood with his back to me, head down and shoulders heaving, hands thrust deep into his pockets, swearing savagely beneath his breath. Kenneth, who never swears.

I shook myself off and sat down on a rock. "Ken," I said, "tell me. Let me share it. Please!"

Ken's voice in torment said, "I can't. I shouldn't."

"Yes, you can." I waited. "I know about Doug's running away."

"Doug!" A world of anguish and lost illusion was in that name. "He lit out, the rotten stinking coward. And left everybody who's been hurt to pick up the pieces! Just the minute he heard—" He stopped.

"I know about Doug and Mary Lou," I said, not moving. "I've known for months. Mary Lou told me. And the rest of it, what's been happening this week—well, I guessed."

Ken turned and looked at me, surprised, and the resistance drained away. "That does make a difference," he admitted.

He dropped down on the ground beside me and began dissecting a blade of elephant grass. "Mr. Hodge came over to the house last night. He was drunk, but not so drunk he didn't know what he was saying. He said Doug had gotten Mary Lou in the family way, and he had to marry her or 'fork over the moolah to get rid of the kid.' His exact words," Ken said bitterly, watching me go numb with shock. "Then he started yelling things at my parents. Terrible things. That they were stinking parents. That they'd raised their brats to think they could do anything they wanted, they were better than everybody else. And that they weren't going to get away with it, not with him, he'd crucify them first. And then Doug—"

Ken swallowed painfully. "Doug laughed! He said he wasn't going to marry the town slut to please anybody. And how did he know it was his kid, anyway? It could be anybody's! After he's been bragging to the fellows for months that he was the only one who'd gotten her to come through!"

"Oh, Ken . . ."

"My God," Ken whispered in wonder. "He *was* my god. All the time we were growing up. He was everything I wanted to be but wasn't, did everything I never had the guts to do." His body began to shake as if he had the chill. "Ever since we were little kids. He was everything, and I was nothing. All I wanted in life was to make him proud of me some day. . . ."

I swallowed hard. "Ken—are you sure you should be telling me all this?"

"Why not?" Kenneth said brutally. "By tonight everybody's going to know the truth. All masks, as Mr. Grimes would say, are off! That poor dumb kid tried to kill herself because of my brother. God, how he could . . . if it were me, I—I'd— But he doesn't either know or care. And that's hell!"

Automatically my arms reached out to him, and I held him,

his head in my lap. "All my life," Ken said slowly, "he's been somebody for me to strive to copy. Oh, I saw his faults, but like Ma, I thought they were just—surface blemishes. Even lately, when I couldn't help seeing more and more—I kept telling myself, maybe he'll get over it, he'll get back to being what I thought he was. But he won't. He never was. I realized that today. He's like the Picture of Dorian Gray. A Prince of Darkness, beautiful on the outside and all rotten inside. And I—I'm a nothing fool who's spent his life trying to be like a dream that never was, because he's not man enough to stand on his own two feet."

"Ken Latham, don't you *ever* say that!" I blazed. "You're not nothing. You're ten times the man he ever will be! Or you wouldn't be here right now, loving him so much, feeling the things that he ought to be feeling! It takes a real man to be able to feel those things—and to be strong enough not to be ashamed to say them!"

And then somehow I was down on the grass beside him, holding him again, and Ken was using my body to cling to, I somehow sensed, kind of like Missy clutched her favorite blanket to ward off nightmare. But it didn't matter, because I knew that for each of us just anybody wouldn't do. Our minds and spirits yearned for each other, for something that we could find nowhere else. We completed each other.

Nothing happened, nothing that I couldn't go home and tell my mother. Yet at the same time, everything happened. We were one in the way of the lovers in that John Donne poem. And I began to understand at last that paradox of the phoenix and the turtle.

> *Two distincts, division none,*
> *Number there in love was slain. . . .*

In some weird way we were one, and at the same time more our selves; we had been enriched and not diminished.

Somehow, in our vulnerability, in our sensitivity to each other's needs, we had stumbled into a gift of grace. And as we walked home in silence, hand in hand, not needing to speak, I felt a deep gratitude to God. And a deep pity for Doug and Mary Lou. Ken and I had gone down into the Valley of the Shadow, and had come up in a kind of spiritual oneness which they, for all their physical union, had never known—which perhaps they never would.

CHAPTER TEN

June

Kenneth and I had crossed a Rubicon. June had come, and I was going to be fifteen. My Keeping Book for the year was almost filled.

"I'll give you a new one for your birthday," Celinda said.

"I wish you would," I said. But even as I spoke I knew I no longer needed it, not in the way I had before. My writing, like myself, had changed. I had to write—and I always would—in order to pass on what I had been given. But no more as a talisman, no more in order to prove something to myself.

"How about an evening party this year?" Mama said one night at dinner. "Been thinking we might move the parlor furniture out so you could dance." I nearly fell out of my seat from shock. And Pa, who'd caught my eye, stared at the ceiling and tried to look innocent.

I figured I'd better get the word around quickly, before Mama changed her mind. Notes were passed in abundance during classes the next day, and after school Celinda and Anne and Stella came over to help me plan. Marnie joined us on the porch for the cake and lemonade, but she bowed out quickly as soon as the work began.

"I'm going to the lot to play ball with Jimmy. You kids can sit here and rack your brains trying to pair people up and make it all come out even. You can have the fun of addressing envelopes and licking stamps. I'll help you move the furniture the day of the party. I may even squeeze lemons for the punch. But that's it."

"You'll come to the party fast enough, and with Jimmy, if Mama'll let you."

"Sure," Marnie said promptly. She looked around at us and grinned wickedly. "You can sit here like ladies figuring out how to get the boys. I'm going out *with* mine, I hope you notice!" She went off, whistling, swinging her catcher's mitt. My sister Marnie, as I may have remarked, is not a fool.

Mama didn't know whether to be troubled or relieved that Marnie still chose to act as if she didn't know she was a girl. "Out there sliding around in dust and mud and hollering like a banshee. She'd be wearing britches if I'd let her. Oh, well, s'pose I ought to be glad it's baseball and not football Jimmy likes. No tackling."

"Mama!"

"Wasn't born yesterday," Mama retorted. "And you're a sight denser than I think you are if you've the notion it's a ball game Marnie's after winning! Saving grace is, that Breidenbach boy's just a big kid if he is fifteen. Still thinks of her as one of the fellows."

I wondered just how much Mama had been noticing lately about Kenneth and me.

So we planned and conspired, and put our heads together after school, and passed more notes whenever we thought the teachers weren't looking. As Marnie predicted, we were having problems making the invitation list come out even—or at least in a way that would keep everybody speaking. If one thing, more than anything else, summed up and underscored the changes that had taken place in the past year, it was the way everyone took for granted that this was going to be a couples' party. Even Celinda did not put up any objections, a fact that Stella and I noted with secret satisfaction. Our problems lay in another direction: who to team with Anne and Junius?

"I'll come alone," Anne said flatly. "Or I'll stay home. Or I'll go along with anybody else you can think of. But I will not be stuck with that unanimated scarecrow for the evening, so don't even think it."

"Oh, you'll come, and not with Junius," Stella said, unruffled. "Maybe Larry and Ben can think of someone."

"I could ask that Felsen boy Ben's been hanging around with lately," I suggested. "He was in the play, so I know him well enough to invite." From the studied casualness with which Anne greeted this suggestion, I was pretty sure she approved of the idea.

That left Junius as the dilemma, and the next afternoon I stopped off at Bronwyn's on my way home to lay the matter before my sister. "You're his stepmother. It's your responsibility to make him halfway human."

"I'm still a bride adjusting to marriage," Bron said virtuously. "I can't be expected to deal with mothering a weird teen-ager!"

I snorted. "You're adjusted fine. You've even got Sourpuss Sadie eating out of your hands, and you know it. How did you do it?"

Bron shrugged. "Have her for dinner once a week, and ask her advice or for a shopping expedition now and then. I guess the poor soul's never been wanted anywhere before. Anyway, Tish, Junius isn't so bad when he's by himself. Especially if we let him have his animals and books." She picked up the orphaned kitten, now half-grown, which was purring seductively around her ankles. "Look at Aphrodite, hasn't she turned out beautiful?"

"She's gorgeous," I said heartlessly. "And you're a genius. And you and Sidney are as happy as a pair of clams. Now will you please tell me what to do with Junius? I can't *not* invite him."

"Let him come alone," Bron said absently. "He'll be happier anyway, and an extra man never hurts. Tish, come see the kitchen. I painted it yesterday, and I've just hung up new curtains."

It was astonishing the difference Bron had brought to that house in six months, and without any major changes. The biggest addition was the brocade draperies in dining room and parlor, and the velvet portieres that draped the connecting arch. Bron ran her hand down them lovingly as we passed. "I suppose I ought to take them down for the summer, but I hate to do it. Can you imagine, Sadie had them packed away in the attic all these years because she thought curtains were unsanitary? I found them in a trunk; Sarah made them." Sarah had been Junius's mother.

I shivered. "Don't you mind having them around?"

"Why should I?" Bron asked simply. "I'm the second Mrs. Albright. And Sarah's a part of what made Sidney what he is, so I should be grateful. Poor old Junius might have turned out better if she'd lived."

By the end of the following week, the party was definitely progressing, and my excitement was not even dimmed by the way Mama was using it as an excuse to rope all of us into one of her housecleaning marathons. I couldn't get it through her head that the kids weren't going to care if the attic hadn't been cleaned or the curtains washed.

"Half of them won't notice you have a new dress, either," Mama retorted, "but I didn't notice that stop you from pestering for one."

I couldn't quite believe that dress myself. It was Mama's birthday present, made of the same lilac voile as the wedding gown I'd worn as Juliet. She had put hours into fine hand-tucking and appliqués of cobweb lace. Its frothing flounces reached my instep, and what was more important, its tight bodice revealed what I'd been noticing for some time now—I was finally beginning to develop curves. I couldn't wait for Ken to see me in it. I wondered what he'd say. Not much, probably; he rarely did, but I loved the way his eyes lighted up. Kenneth could use some things to light him up.

Doug and Mary Lou were not coming to the party. Nobody had seen Doug or Mary Lou for weeks. A few days after that awful Saturday, it had been given out that Mary Lou had had a breakdown from overwork and gone away to her grandmother's to recover. And the neighborhood, which ordinarily would have laughed itself silly at the notion of Mary Lou overstudying, accepted the story and let the matter drop. Pretty soon Mrs. Hodge had started dropping hints that she might be having a new arrival at her age.

"You were right," Stella whispered when she heard the rumor. "I wouldn't have believed it."

"I've lived here longer'n you," I murmured darkly. "I know what we're like." It wasn't easy knowledge to accept.

No one had seen Doug Latham again. Not even his family, and that was why Kenneth hurt. The Lathams were like my family, they had a tight inner dignity and a pride that says you do not cry in public, so nobody saw Mrs. Latham without her customary look of gentle poise and her chin up high, or

Mr. Latham without his too-humorous affability and jovial grin. Everybody whispered and wondered, but the neighborhood didn't know what was going on behind those stiffly starched lace curtains. I did. I knew every heartbeat of the breathless week that intervened before Mrs. Latham got a letter from her brother in Pennsylvania, saying that Doug was there. I knew what agony it was for Ken to go to school each day and face the knowing eyes, the rumors. I knew how his father had forbidden Doug's name to be mentioned or any letters written, and how his mother cried. And when my family, too, speculated and gossipped at the dinner table, I didn't say a word.

"I don't know how long he'll stay there," Kenneth told me. "Doug hates the country. Just as much as he hated school. He's apt to just bum around from city to city, hopping freights." He was silent for a long moment. "I wanted to go back to my uncle's this summer," he said at last. "I loved it there. Now—I don't know. For a lot of reasons."

"Maybe," I said carefully, "Mama would let me go back to spend the summer with Gramps again. I loved it, too."

"I wish you could," Kenneth said. "I swear to God, sometimes I almost envy Doug. I wish we could just run away together and be ourselves! But we're not Dougs."

It was at that particular moment I started being determined my birthday party would be a Keeping Day, a talisman of all that had been good of the past year, all I wished in the future for Ken, and Celinda, and Stella, and Anne, and everyone I loved. It started becoming almost an article of faith.

By the middle of the party week, Mama was in a swivet but the house was shining. Celinda reported that her father had bought her a store-bought party dress, her first. Stella was making her own; she had caught the sewing bug from Anne and was stitching up a storm. Ben had located the Japanese lanterns in the attic; he planned to string them all around the porch. We'd started carting the least necessary furniture to the attic. Mama's cutwork tablecloth hung from a clothesline up there too, so its perfection would not be marred by a single crease. I had put tall candles in the bronze candelabra with their crystal prisms, and in Grandma Stryker's silver candlesticks. I planned to make the parlor a bower of roses—masses of crimson rambler, and the tiny sweet-scented white ones, and Mama's silvery-pink roses with their poignant fragrance.

Bronwyn was helping Mama in the refreshment department, and she was also lending us the cut-glass punch bowl she'd gotten as a wedding present. Aunt Kate sniffed about that, but Mama just sniffed right back. "Children growing up. Have right to nice things," she said. She looked Kate right in the eye. "Treat 'em like babies too long, no social graces, turn out like Junius Albright." At which point Aunt Kate shut up, since her dear friend Sourpuss Sadie had been responsible for that fiasco.

I'd taken Bron's advice and was letting Junius come to the party alone, probably to his great relief. Mike Felsen had accepted his invitation, so Anne was happy. And even Celinda, calling up to describe the glories of the new party dress, had hesitated and then added softly, "Tish? I'm awfully glad you're having this party," before hanging up.

In school, classes were reaching that end-of-term condition we all knew well. Everybody was hustling to get last assignments and projects done, or groaning over exams that no one intended to study for anyway. School would close with a half-session the Wednesday following my birthday; our small group planned to stay after to help Mr. Grimes and Mrs. Owens close up their rooms, and then have a picnic. People were beginning to talk about vacation plans. Ken still didn't know what he was going to do.

Two days before the party, I emerged from the cloakroom before school to see Ken coming towards me down the hall. I knew at once that something was wrong. His face had that tight, shuttered, walling-the-world-off look. I fell into step beside him, cursing the fact that we were in school and the nine o'clock bell about to ring. I knew how to knock Ken's walls down, but I couldn't do it there. "Ken," I whispered, hurrying to keep up with his rapid stride, "what's happened?"

"Later. We can't talk here."

The little muscle in his face had begun to flicker, so I plunged on. "What is it? Please tell me. Is it Doug?"

"Tish, I said not now! Let me be!"

I took one look at his taut chin and shut my mouth.

We had no uninterrupted chance to talk all day, but as we walked to classes, and in the ones we had together, I could feel the tension build. At last three o'clock came, and the mob swarmed out. I pulled Ken into Mrs. Owens's empty classroom and shut the door. "Ken, what is it?"

Ken faced me. "We've had another letter from my uncle. Doug's run off again. This time God alone knows where."

"God will take care of him," I said, and did not add that Doug had an uncanny ability for always landing on his feet no matter who else was hurt.

"It's just about killed my mother. Tish, she's turning into an old woman overnight. Lord only knows what he's up to— or what he'll live on—out West, in a city somewhere, hopping freights. . . . He could get killed." I knew what Ken was thinking, that Doug would do anything he could or chose to do, and would never think of the consequences for himself or anyone else.

Ken swung away to stare out the window, hands thrust

deep into his pockets. I sat on a desk and looked at his rigid back and ached. What I wanted to do was go and throw my arms around him and hold him tight. But something—wisdom, or chickenheartedness—held me back. For this time his control had not broken; he could hate me for making it do so, hate himself for needing me and for my seeing. And so I sat, and when Ken said brusquely, "I've got to get home," and walked out rapidly, I did not follow. I went home, and plunged into party preparations, and cried inside.

The party, oh, the party—I knew that in some mystic way I was using it as a talisman, counting on it to set all things right. At least it would give Kenneth a couple of happy hours.

Bron came up right after supper to confer with Mama about cake recipes. Pa was moving more furniture, muttering "Tarnation foolishness," and enjoying the whole thing, and Ben and Marnie were making stabs at helping while arguing about the relative merits of their favorite baseball teams. Missy was getting into everything, chattering a mile a minute, and Katie was chewing happily on a crust of bread and pulling Cicero's ears. Nobody noticed that I was very quiet. I thought about Doug, and Mary Lou, and the look on Kenneth's face, and prayed that the party would be a Keeping Day.

The telephone rang in the midst of this. "I'll answer it," Bron said, and picked up the receiver. I heard her say, "Yes, this is Bronwyn Sterling. It's Bronwyn Albright now. Who? Mr. *Stanyon*?" Her voice changed. "Oh. Yes. Yes, of course. Just a minute." She gestured frantically for paper and pencil, and Pa passed them to her. The whole kitchen had fallen silent, arrested by her tone. She scribbled rapidly, interspersing the silences with terse sentences in her odd, crisp, grown-up voice. "Thank you—very much. We'll be in touch. I'll call you back tonight."

She hung up the phone and turned slowly, while we held

our breaths. "That was Mr. Stanyon," she said unnecessarily. "The minister out by Gramps's." She looked at our parents. "Gramps was trying to get that big stump out of the yard this morning. The roots went deeper than he thought, and he had to tug and pull. You know Gramps. He was determined it wasn't going to lick him." She stopped. "He had a heart attack. He's dead."

Nobody spoke.

"Mr. Stanyon took care of everything with the undertaker there," Bron said. "He says if you want, after folks pay their respects there tomorrow morning, he'll have the—body shipped here by train. He says we ought to have the funeral day after tomorrow."

"That's my birthday party," I said in a voice I scarcely knew.

"Can't be helped. Party's off anyway, acourse," Mama said automatically.

"*No.*" I didn't know I was going to say it, I didn't even know where my own voice came from as everybody swung around and goggled at me. "No. It can't be off. Gramps is dead. We can't bring him back. And we've got to have the party."

"That any child of mine . . ." Mama said slowly. "Selfish. No heart." Tears fought in her stern eyes, and she got up and stumped out of the room, and Pa followed.

Missy, seeming to feel that it was needed, started to cry, and that started Katie. Marnie picked her up and rocked her, staring at me grimly. Bron turned to the telephone. "I'll call Sidney. We'll have to talk to the funeral director, and Mr. Derbyshire at church. And call Aunt Annie, she'll want to come down."

"I'll go over and tell Aunt Kate," Ben said, and left.

I wandered out onto the front porch, now veiled in twilight, and the fragrance of Mama's roses assailed me. I leaned my head against the post where the wisteria vines sent up their gnarled old trunk, and my body ached, and my eyes were dry. And I was filled with an awful emptiness. Gramps was an old man, and he was dead, and I was never going to see him again, and it simply didn't matter to me at all. I couldn't even remember what he looked like. And I wasn't going to be able to share with Kenneth the longed-for Keeping Day.

Ben must have gone over to Molloys' after he left Aunt Kate's, because in school the next morning Stella knew, and that was a blessing. "I'll tell the kids about the party for you," she said, "so you won't have to."

"All right."

Stella glanced at me oddly, but said nothing, and I had an idea that in a queer sort of way she understood. Nobody else did, that was sure. Very little penetrated through my daze, but that fact did. It showed in the quality of Mama's stoic silence, which was different towards me than towards the others. Everybody ignored me, and I ignored everybody else. I could have talked to Kenneth, but we were walled off from each other by the busywork of funeral preparations, by the constant stream of well-meaning, platitude-spouting grown-up friends.

The furniture was put back in the parlor. People kept arriving with cakes, with salads, with bowls of chicken soup. Bron packed much of it up to carry off to her house, for she was going to have everyone back to her house for the meal after the funeral. I went with her to help carry and to help her with the tidying up.

Flowers kept coming, stiff, artificial-looking bouquets Gramps would have snorted at, and I hated them. Mr. Albright drove down to the station with the funeral director to meet the coffin, and that evening there were visiting hours in our parlor, and the candles I'd put out for the party were lit, and the neighborhood streamed in and out, saying artificial things. The kids came; many of them had liked Gramps, and they wanted to show their support to Ben and Marnie and me. Ken was there, but we couldn't talk, and it wasn't only because of lack of privacy.

Mama and Aunt Kate had a public row, because Aunt Kate thought Missy ought to be made to look at Gramps in the coffin, and Mama wouldn't have it. "Too young. Not the way I want her to remember him. Don't fight me, Kate!"

I looked, because I couldn't find a way to avoid it, but it wasn't Gramps. It was some stranger whom I'd never known.

Finally, thank God, everyone went home, and the coffin was closed and taken to church for the funeral service, and we went to bed. I don't know whether anybody slept. The next morning everybody acted drugged. At least nobody was bursting in and out. The family had forgotten about my birthday, and I didn't care. We sat around the kitchen table drinking stale coffee and thinking our private thoughts. At last Pa pushed back his chair and rose.

"We'd better get dressed. Have to leave for the funeral in half an hour."

We started to follow, and all of a sudden out of nowhere, as before, I heard my own voice say, "No."

"No what?" Mama asked evenly.

"No funeral. That's not Gramps down there. I don't know where he is, I've lost him, but he's not there. I just can't go, that's all."

"Suit yourself," Mama said. "Don't care, I'm sure." She walked out, and I walked out, too, up to my room and shut the door.

It was opened a few minutes later by Marnie, who stood

regarding me coldly from the doorway. "Just what do you think you're doing?" she inquired.

"What do you mean?"

"You know darn well what I mean. Dramatizing poor little misunderstood sensitive Letitia." Marnie stared at me, her eyes bright with tears. "How could you, Tish? You were always Gramps's favorite, long as I can remember. All of us loved him, but you were special."

"I don't care. I can't help it. And that's the God's truth."

"Then couldn't you at least have pretended, for Mama's sake?" Marnie asked harshly. "You're the one that's supposed to be such a great actress."

"Don't you ever say that to me!"

"Why not?" Marnie retorted. "You've pretended enough at other times, goodness knows. All that stuff about how sensitive you are, and how your feelings are deeper than other folks'! You're a great big no-feeling phoney!"

I couldn't speak, for there was nothing to say. I picked up the hairbrush off the bureau and threw it at her. And in that moment I knew that no matter what it cost me, I was never going to put on another offstage act for as long as I lived.

Somewhere, deep inside my frozen consciousness, I wanted to laugh. It was so funny, I was a good enough actress that when I *was* acting everybody believed it was real, but when I was absolutely honest people always thought I was putting on an act.

Out in the hall a quiet voice said, "That's enough, Marnie," and Marnie looked at my father and flushed and ran away. Pa came in, and shut the door, and stood contemplating me, and I turned away towards the window and wished that I could cry.

"I won't say anything," Pa said finally. "There's not much I can, and you don't much want to hear it anyway. I just wanted you to know that *I'm* not scolding. And I wanted to give you this."

I turned. "What is it?" Pa was holding out an oddly wrapped package, tied with string.

"It's your birthday present from your grandfather," Pa said. "Mr. Stanyon found it sitting on his kitchen table and sent it along. I thought you might like to look at it while we're gone." He set it on the bed, and left, shutting the door behind him.

I didn't reach for it. I sat down in the window seat and heard the rustle of skirts, and muffled voices, and shutting doors as the family left for church. The house grew still. It would be hours before they were back, I knew. I was still in my kimono, and after a while I got up and dressed, avoiding the dark clothes I was supposed to have worn to the funeral, trying not to look at the lavender birthday dress. I thought of Kenneth, and wondered what he was doing, and could hardly evoke his face. I thought of Gramps, and could remember nothing. I felt as if it were I who was dead.

Presently I went over to the bed, picked up the odd package, and pulled the string. But all that fell out was a pile of brittle papers and old envelopes. They had a musty smell, as if they'd been long dead. And all at once I had to get outside, into fresh air and sunlight. I bundled the papers together and ran outdoors, across the small strip of lawn, up into our old tree house. I hadn't been there yet this spring, but suddenly I had a need to go back to this relic of my childhood. Several great crumpled leaves from last autumn lay on the floor, and the sun filtered through this year's young green leaves. I sat down on the floor with the papers in my lap and picked up the one that looked the newest.

"Dear Tish," said my grandfather's great illegible scrawl, "I found these in the attic and calculate they can give more to you than me. I'm old now, and anyway I don't need them.

But you understand a lot more than folks have bargained for, and you're going to be a writer. I'd like you to have these, and use them in a book some day if you've a mind to, and dispose of them any way that you see fit. I'd hate to have them forgotten or laughed over—can't figure out which would be worse. At any rate, you won't laugh, and you'll understand them some day, if you don't now. This is kind of like giving you a part of myself. Who knows, maybe some day when you're a famous writer you'll make me immortal! All my love," and he signed it, not *Gramps,* but with his full name, *Cornelius Van Zandt Stryker.* It's funny, I'd never thought of him that way.

I picked up an envelope and drew out its brittle contents. The paper and ink were yellow and brown with age. A spidery feminine writing I'd never seen began, *"My dearest love . . ."*

They were all there, all the letters and notes my grandparents had ever exchanged, since they first were courting and she had come to Pennsylvania, a very young and pretty New England Puritan, to teach in a one-room school. I saw the letters progress from stiff, shy fumblings to the gradual unfolding Kenneth and I had known, the ability to share one's secret thoughts in a private language. I found out what I'd never understood before, how my farmer grandfather had come to know so much about books. He'd learned it from my grandmother, who'd been classics trained. I even found the John Donne poem Kenneth had read to me, and the lines from Wordsworth Gramps had quoted.

> *Though nothing can bring back the hour*
> *Of splendour in the grass, of glory in the flower;*
> *We will grieve not, rather find*
> *Strength in what remains behind.*

There were letters, notes, Christmas cards, scrawled messages and bits of poems, spanning nearly forty years. I scarcely remembered my grandmother except as a plump motherly figure. Now she began to emerge from her letters as a person as young as I, at once a stranger and part of my blood and bone. And with her, holding her hand, a tall young man, a little like Ken was now, but with Gramps's mischievous, knowing eyes. She was Evie Letitia Chambers Stryker, and she was shy, and half-afraid of the life she was rushing headlong into. She had married at sixteen. She too had lain, as I had, in a flowery meadow, held tight by the man she loved too soon. And I understood why Gramps had wanted me to have these letters; and why he had been afraid that folks would laugh, or worse, forget; and why he had understood my pain the night of *Romeo and Juliet*.

When I finished reading, the sun had started its downward curve and sent golden fingers through the green branches. I awoke as from a dream to find myself sitting on the floor of the tree house with the hum of bees and the song of the thrush drifting up from the Queen Anne's Lace, and all at once I knew what it was I had to do. I folded the letters carefully and tucked them inside the bodice of my dress. Then I went into the house, strangely empty and silent in the afternoon. I took a candle from the silver candlesticks on the sideboard, the candlesticks that Great-Great-Grandmother Stryker had been given as a bride. I went out the front door, down the steps, down the street the few blocks to where Grace Church stood, always open, on its familiar corner.

The pale grey dimness reached out to welcome me as the door swung shut behind me. No one was there, but the stillness was full of a thousand presences of people who had been christened and confirmed and married and buried there back through the years, and of something else, something that was the sum total of it all and yet infinitely more. I lit my taper from the altar candle and, shielding the frail flame in my hand, I walked with it out of the church, along the streets humming with the familiar sounds of summer afternoon. The flame flickered but burned on gallantly.

Once in the back garden, I knelt and stood the candle carefully in the earth. Then one by one I fed my grandparents' letters into the flame, watching the pale brittle paper turn grey, and shrivel, and fall into ashes in a symbolism I sensed but couldn't put into words. The thrush was singing again, and over in the columbine a pale gold butterfly quivered motionless on a crimson flower. I remembered Peter's saying, "That's a *citheronia regalis*," and I heard my grandfather's voice quoting Wordsworth, and saw again the young-old eyes burning in his weathered face. And at last the tight band in my chest loosened, and I was able to cry.

I cried not for the old man who had died, for the grandfather whom I had loved, whom I would always love. I was crying for a young man and a girl who had met and kissed in a flowery meadow, who had covenanted together for good or ill, who had lived and loved and wept and laughed together, who had known the shriveling and breaking of the body that was only the shell, the cocoon that held the invincible, unconquerable human spirit that was within. The spirit that would always be young, and the love that was eternal.

I wept with my face pressed in the dark, warm-scented earth, pulsing with life, and the bees hummed, and the candle flame flickered in the afternoon sunlight. *Continuity, continuity,* winked the flame. *I am the Resurrection and the Life. . . .*

A shadow fell across the grass, and then Kenneth knelt beside me. He didn't say a word, just put his arms around me and lifted me and held me close, so close that again I could feel our two hearts beating. He knelt there and held me for a long, long time, until my sobbing ceased and the candle guttered and went out in a little pool of wax and a tracery of ashes.

I straightened and wiped my stinging eyes on my sleeve, not knowing what to say, not needing to speak. Almost involuntarily, our eyes met, without defenses. I love you, Kenneth, I thought. And one day we too will grow old and die. And in between there will be times when we too will know the humdrum of routine and surface living, which is a kind of death. But inside, inside we will always share this Keeping Day, and be as young together as we are now. We will always have this, all the days of our lives, and perhaps even more.

Looking into Kenneth's eyes was like looking into bottomless blue pools that have depths beyond depths. We weren't touching, but our eyes clung together the way our bodies had, moments before. I realized I was trembling.

Suddenly, from deep within us both, laughter welled up, like a dam bursting. We rolled on the grass like children, lost together in the blessed, sweet, painful, sacramental laughter. Then Kenneth sprang to his feet and stood grinning down at me, himself once more. He cast a long shadow. He held out his hand to pull me up and we ran together, still laughing, into the sunlight. Behind us the golden butterfly rose and spiraled towards the sun.

Excerpts from
THE SANCTUARY TREE
by
Norma Johnston
Coming from ACE TEMPO in January

Somehow holidays are always cataclysmic around our household, and I must have been out of my mind to think this Fourth of July would be an exception. I did try; I'd swear on a stack of Bibles that I tried, and I honestly think that Mama did as well. I suppose it was just the nature of the beast, as Gramps used to say, that human nature got in the way of intended sainthood. Gramps. I hadn't meant to start thinking about him again.

Gramps, unlike Mama, would have understood about the Fourth. Joy and sorrow, frustration and despair—well, yes, tears and anger and cusswords, too—we ran the gamut. And the words to describe me, myself, are "in a fog."

Maybe I need to be in a fog for a time until my heart grows quiet. And maybe it's even good for my soul that Mama goes around sniffing, "Not quite as grown up as you think you are, young lady, and don't you forget it." There are times, especially when I am with Kenneth, when I feel half as old as time.

"Tish Sterling and Kenneth Latham are sweethearts." That's what everyone in our neighborhood of the Bronx is saying. Some of the grownups unfortunately even add an audible, "Isn't that cute?" And the unbelievable part of it is that neither I nor Kenneth even care.

"They're goopy about each other," is the way my younger sister Marnie puts it. And then, I'm afraid, my temper does snap.

There are times—also when I am with Kenneth —when I'm very conscious that we're both fifteen, when I feel that I'm skating on very thin ice indeed, and over a seething whirlpool, to boot.

* * *

It was a lovely evening, and a happy one, and I almost forgot the shadows that were brooding around the edges of my mind. I remembered them in church next morning, though, because Kenneth wasn't there. He must have gone somewhere with his family, for he didn't appear all that day, nor the next. Mama kept us all hopping on Monday with ironing, packing, last-minute tidying up, but during the lunch hour, and after work and dinner I kept watching for Kenneth's face, listening for his whistle.

He didn't come. Day dragged into hot evening and to night, and he still did not appear.

"Ought to be in bed. Got to get an early start tomorrow," Mama said firmly at eleven thirty. Mr. Albright was coming by for us at a quarter to eight.

I didn't mean to sleep, and yet I must have, for before I knew it, the sun was streaming in and Marnie was hollering in the door, "Better get a move on. Mama's jumping like a June bug on a griddle."

"All right. I'm coming."

Marnie regarded me unsympathetically. "If you're going to keep on mooning like that from here on in, it's going to be a miserable summer."

I bit back a retort, and I kept my tongue firmly under control all through breakfast, which was pretty hectic. Actually, I did not hear too much of the commotion; my eyes were on the door. Ken would come, he was bound to, he wouldn't let me go with no good-bye.

*   *   *

Presently people started drifting off, murmuring things about having to be out in the fields early in the morning. Mama and Aunt Annie settled on the side lawn with Mr. and Mrs. Beeson, who were talking about the modernizations they had in mind. Indoor plumbing and hot water would be a definite improvement, but something very special and unique would be gone.

Something that had made the farm a sanctuary to me had long since vanished. And that thing was Gramps's vital, living presence. I would have that, from now on, only in my heart. It had been folly for me to think a geographical entity had anything to do with it. Oh, Mama had known that, hadn't she, all along? That was why she had been able to look with stony equanimity on those wagons driving off with all the bits and pieces of what once had been a home. What had been stripped in the auction today was nothing but the shell.

And it came to me that, drat it all, maybe Mr. Stanyon had been right, that to hold onto a husk, to delude oneself that the breath of life could still be in it, was a blasphemy and an idolatry. The only constant in life was change. No, there was more. There were also memories. And love.

I had not found sanctuary here, because sanctuary was not a geographical location. I had to find it—and wasn't that what Gramps had always been trying to teach me—in myself. And in kindred people, like Gramps himself. And Ken.

* * *

I'd thought things would get better once summer vacation started. But they didn't. Nothing seems to work out the way it's supposed to, any more. Mary Lou's having a baby, and Doug Latham has run away, and Ken, who knows exactly what his brother is and loves him anyway, has gone through hell. I was counting on my birthday party in June to break through the wall of Kenneth's numbness, but the day of my intended party turned instead into the day of Gramps's funeral, and since that time we've both been walking round in a state of frozen suspended animation. Except when we're alone together, except when we end up locked in each other's arms. Which even I realize uneasily, deep down, is not—suitable. But it's too late. Kenneth and I have been through too much, have come too far, and there's no going back. There's never any going back, no matter how you want to; that's what this summer's teaching me. That's why I feel this need to strike out at something, someone, in helpless anger.